Lost in Gator Swamp

Dusty and Frank went to the lakeshore and slid the hydroplane off the grass and into the water.

"Here's your chance," Dusty said, pointing to the pilot's seat. "Ready to try a takeoff?"

"Sure." Frank climbed into the pilot's seat and quickly reviewed the controls and flying procedures. He started the engine and began his takeoff run.

Frank felt the plane lift off the surface of the water. He aimed the nose of the plane for the tops of the trees bordering the lake. Frank gasped as the plane barely cleared the treetops, but Dusty just gave an excited holler.

That was when Frank heard the engine sputter. The engine sputtered again and then cut off.

The nose began to dip. The plane was going down!

The Hardy Boys Mystery Stories

Available from MINSTREL Books

THE HARDY BOYS®

142

LOST IN GATOR SWAMP

FRANKLIN W. DIXON

A MINSTREL® BOOK

Published by POCKET BOOKS

New York   London   Toronto   Sydney   Tokyo   Singapore

A MINSTREL PAPERBACK *Original*

 A Minstrel Book published by
POCKET BOOKS, a division of Simon & Schuster Inc.
1230 Avenue of the Americas, New York, NY 10020

Copyright © 1997 by Simon & Schuster Inc.

Front cover illustration by Lee MacLeod

Produced by Mega-Books, Inc.

ISBN: 0-671-00054-3

First Minstrel Books printing February 1997

10 9 8 7 6 5 4 3 2 1

THE HARDY BOYS MYSTERY STORIES is a trademark of Simon & Schuster Inc.

THE HARDY BOYS, A MINSTREL BOOK and colophon are registered trademarks of Simon & Schuster Inc.

Printed in the U.S.A.

Contents

1 Flying to the Everglades

"Watch those trees!" Joe Hardy shouted as the hydroplane buzzed over an island of mangroves, nearly grazing the top branches.

"Yee-haw!" Dusty Cole hollered, pulling up the nose of his small aircraft. "I didn't really scare you, did I, Joe?"

"No, Mr. Cole, not really," Joe replied, pushing back his blond hair and wiping the sweat off his brow.

"Dusty is a daredevil even when he's not riding rodeo," Chet Morton shouted over the roar of the engine. Chet and Frank Hardy were squeezed into the backseat of the plane.

Chet had been invited by his friend Dusty Cole to attend the Swampland Rodeo that was to take place over the weekend, and he had asked Frank and Joe to come with him. Right now they were headed for Dusty's remote fishing camp, where they would stay during the rodeo.

A flock of white birds took flight as the hydroplane approached one of the thousands of islands that dotted the Everglades in southern Florida.

"Egrets!" Frank shouted. He glanced at the travel book he had brought with him from the Bayport Library.

"Anyone else hungry?" Chet asked, stuffing a handful of potato chips into his mouth. "It may be the last real food we'll eat for a while."

"You'd better slow down, Chet," Joe said with a smile, "or you won't be able to pull yourself up into the saddle for the steer-roping competition."

"It's okay. These are those new low-fat chips," Chet explained between crunches. "So I figure I can eat twice as many."

"We'll stock up on grub at the Swampland Trading Post," Dusty assured them as the plane began the descent, heading toward a large pond in the middle of the sprawling swampland.

"This is like landing on huge water skis," Frank said as he looked at the water below.

"That's right," Dusty said. "Hydroplanes have runners instead of wheels. The runners, or pontoons, can float very much like water skis."

Dusty skipped the pontoons along the surface

2

of the water and then glided toward the Swampland Trading Post, which was just a wooden shack perched at the water's edge. It was a combination general store, boat- and horse-renting outfit, and the only commercial establishment in Gator Swamp.

The second that Chet was on solid ground, he pulled a rope from his duffel bag and lassoed a dock post. "I've been practicing on parking meters back in Bayport. I'm ready to rope some steer."

"Ever since you met Chet and his dad at that rodeo they attended in Wyoming last summer," Frank told Dusty, "Chet's gone cowboy crazy."

"He's come to the right place," Dusty replied.

As the group was stepping onto the front porch of the store, angry shouts erupted from the direction of the parking lot. Frank spotted a Native American man with long gray hair holding a hunting knife against the neck of a policewoman.

"Move and I'll cut your throat!" The man growled his threat.

"Hey, put it down! Are you nuts?" Joe cried out as he and the others rushed toward the scene.

Seeing them coming on the run, the man released the officer. "Dusty Cole!" he called out cheerfully. "How are you?"

"Great, just great!" Dusty replied as the group approached.

"Wait a second," Joe said. "You know this guy?"

3

"Who, Angus? For twenty-some years," Dusty said, slapping the man's shoulder. "I've known Angus Tallwalker ever since he opened the Swampland Trading Post."

"What were you just doing?" Frank asked Tallwalker, still confused.

"I was just showing Deputy Miles how one of the robbers held a knife to my throat," Tallwalker replied, slipping his knife back into its sheath.

"You were robbed?" Joe asked.

"Yup," Tallwalker said. "Two robbers broke into a bank vault in Miami a couple of days ago—the day the big storm hit us. Got away with half a million dollars. The police had a roadblock waiting here at Frog's Peninsula."

"What does that have to do with you?" Dusty broke in.

"Well, if you clam up long enough, I'll tell you," Tallwalker said, ribbing his friend. "To avoid the roadblock, the robbers turned into the trading post, ditched their car, and stole one of my airboats at knife point."

"An airboat can motor right through the saw grass in only a few inches of water," Dusty explained. "A fan pushes the boat right along the surface."

Deputy Miles, who had been waiting patiently, now tapped her pencil on her notepad. "Let's get on with the investigation. You were telling me that you never got a look at the robbers, is that right?" she asked Tallwalker.

"No. They were wearing black hoods," Tallwalker replied.

"Have they found the robbers' boat?" Frank wondered.

"You mean *my* boat," Tallwalker corrected.

"No," Frank said. "I mean *their* boat. This place is called Frog's Peninsula, right?" Tallwalker nodded. "So, we're surrounded on three sides by water," Frank continued. "If the crooks drove out onto the peninsula, then they would have reached a dead end unless they had a boat waiting for them."

Deputy Miles raised her eyebrows. "Good point. I'll be sure I look into that," she said, making a note on her pad. "Do you read a lot of mysteries?"

"*Read* them," Chet cut in. "Frank and Joe *solve* mysteries! They've helped the police in our hometown of Bayport crack dozens of tough cases, and I've been a tremendous asset—"

"But we're all on vacation right now," Joe interrupted, trying to stop Chet before he could say any more. The Hardys preferred not to tell too many people what they did, in case they needed to go under cover.

The radio in the squad car crackled, and Deputy Miles leaned in to take the call. "That was the Coast Guard. They just found your stolen airboat," she said.

"Where?" Tallwalker asked.

"Sunk at the bottom of Florida Bay, I'm afraid," Deputy Miles replied. "The boat must have capsized in the storm. That far from shore, with the ten-foot-high waves and the strong undertow, there's no way the robbers could have survived."

Deputy Miles got into her squad car. "I'd appreciate it if you'd keep this to yourselves," she continued. "We don't want the whole world hunting in Florida Bay for half a million dollars in stolen loot."

After the squad car was gone, Frank said, "Judging from the map in my book, Florida Bay is huge."

"Yep. It's really almost part of the Gulf of Mexico," Dusty said.

"Why would the robbers take a little airboat out on the open sea in a squall?" Frank asked. "They must have known it would capsize."

"Maybe they were trying to reach an island," Joe offered. "Or they could have been heading all the way to Cuba."

"People do crazy things when they're desperate," Dusty remarked. "But we've got our own fish to fry. Frank, you come with me and Angus to the stable yonder." Dusty pointed to a long, narrow wooden shed across the dirt parking lot. He pulled a slip of paper from his pocket. "Joe, here's a shopping list. You go into the store and start stocking up. And Chet—" Dusty turned to the spot where Chet had been standing, but Chet was gone.

Joe spotted Chet in the junkyard next to the parking lot, practicing his lassoing skills on the side mirror of an old rusted car.

The bell on the door jingled as Joe entered the general store. He began placing canned goods on the counter to take to the fishing camp. The bell jingled behind him, and Joe turned to see a tall muscular man with red hair and a scruffy red beard standing in the doorway.

"Do you sell snorkeling equipment?" the red-haired man asked in a deep voice.

"I'm not sure," Joe replied. "Is there any place to snorkel in a swamp?"

Joe was trying to be funny, but the red-haired man did not smile. "I'm going to Key West," he muttered.

"Key West?" Joe asked. "That's a hundred miles from here."

The red-haired man sneered. "Do you have snorkeling equipment or not?"

"I don't work here," Joe replied. "But I think I saw some stuff on those shelves," he added, turning to the back of the store.

Joe heard the bell jingle behind him. When he turned around, the red-haired man was gone. What's his hurry? Joe thought to himself, then decided to follow the man outside to find out.

Joe caught sight of the man boarding an airboat at the end of the dock. Another man stood in the boat, but his back was to Joe. Joe couldn't make out any features, but he could see that the man wore a white cowboy hat with a curled brim and a black-and-orange feather in the band.

Joe heard the red-haired man grumble angrily, "This is never going to work." Joe walked down to the dock to get a better look at the other man's face, when something suddenly wrapped around his ankle. Joe found himself falling head over heels into the swamp.

2 The Man in the White Hat

Joe splashed into the salty, murky swamp water.

"I'm sorry, Joe!" Chet offered Joe a hand up onto the dock and removed the rope noose from Joe's ankle. "I wanted to practice on a moving target, and you were the closest thing to a steer I could find."

"Thanks for the honor, Chet," Joe shot at his friend. "Next time, spare me. I'm soaked!"

Frank came rushing from the direction of the stable. "Are you all right, Joe?"

"Yeah," Joe replied. "Some guy with a red beard came into the store wanting to buy snorkeling equipment. He said he was headed to Key West. I told him I didn't work here, and bam, he was gone.

9

He got into an airboat with a man in a white hat with an orange-and-black feather."

Joe peered across the water, trying to block the glaring morning sun with his hand. "There they are!"

The airboat was heading up a narrow creek and disappeared behind some trees.

"Wow, they must have been in a hurry," Frank remarked.

"Surprise!" Dusty called out. The boys turned to see Dusty and Angus Tallwalker leading two horses and a mule from the stable.

"As long as you've come all this way," Dusty said, "I figured you should be real cowboys. Angus is loaning them to you for the weekend."

Tallwalker nodded toward the gray horse. "His name is Stonewall, and this is Paint Can." The second horse was a white pinto covered with small brown spots.

The mule brayed loudly. "Sorry about Old Caloosa," Tallwalker said, patting the ancient mule on the neck. "But with all the people here for the rodeo, he's the last animal left in my stable."

"That's okay, Mr. Tallwalker," Joe assured him. "Horseback or muleback, we're happy to have the chance to ride."

"You can ride them from here to the rodeo this afternoon," Dusty said. "Right now, I need to get you and our groceries out to the fishing camp. We've got a lot of hungry guests waiting."

Ten minutes later the hydroplane was touching down near a small island located at the point where Gator Swamp emptied into Florida Bay. "It's called Cole's Key, named after my great-grandfather, who settled here a hundred years ago," Dusty said proudly.

A dozen cabins on stilts were scattered along the eastern shore of the sandy crescent-shaped key. The northern end of the small, low island was covered with dense saw grass.

"Welcome to Cole's Fishing Camp," Dusty said as he tied the plane to its mooring on the floating dock. "Everybody told me I was crazy to build a fishing camp here, but the true enthusiasts seem to have found me."

"I understand why you built it here," Joe said, looking around. "This is one of the most peaceful places I've ever seen."

The peacefulness was suddenly broken by the sound of a shotgun blast.

"What was that?" Chet asked.

"It must be Homer Janes, my caretaker," Dusty said, sounding worried. "He owns a shotgun, but I don't know what he would be shooting at."

"We'd better find out," Frank said, as they all headed toward the sound of the blast.

The saw grass was as thick as a meadow of wheat and seven feet high in some places. Once in it, Frank couldn't see a thing.

"Help!" a voice cried. The jagged edges of the long blades nicked Frank's arms as he pushed through the saw grass toward the voice.

Frank came upon a man in a small rowboat, holding a smoking shotgun. He had a short gray beard and was shaking like a leaf.

"Homer!" Dusty called to the man as he and Chet caught up.

"Alligator!" the man exclaimed, pointing to one half of a splintered wooden oar in his boat. "It had teeth like razors. Must have been fifteen feet long. One eye was big, white, and ugly."

"That oar's good for nothing now. We're not far from shore. We'll pull you through this saw grass and back to safety, pronto." Dusty said.

Once on land, Frank and the others turned back, half expecting to see a giant alligator pursuing them through the saw grass. But the water was still. Then Frank noticed something strange in the distance. On a neighboring island were two cypress trees standing side by side and identical in size. Sitting high in the branches of one of these trees was a lone figure, who appeared to be watching them.

"Dusty, does anyone live on the next island?" Frank asked.

Dusty followed Frank's gaze. "You mean on

12

Twin Cypress Key? No, not for a hundred years. Why?"

"Because there's someone—" Frank had only taken his eye off the tree for a moment. But in that time the figure had disappeared.

"Well, there was someone there a second ago, sitting up in the branches of that cypress."

"That's probably Weird Reuben," Homer replied.

"Who?" Frank asked.

"He's a strange one who—" Homer started.

"He's not strange, except to you and some of your tale-telling friends," Dusty said hotly. "Reuben is Angus Tallwalker's grandson," he explained to the others. "I'll admit he's not very sociable. But he's not strange. He lives off the land—by the old ways, like his ancestors did. He doesn't like all the fishermen and tourists who have started overrunning the area. Twin Cypress Key was a special island to his people."

"Wait a second," Frank said, looking around. "Where's Joe?" The younger Hardy was nowhere in sight.

"Joe!" Chet yelled. "Where are you?"

"I'm over here!" Joe called back. "The question is, where are you?"

Joe had set out a minute after the others had gone to investigate the shotgun blast and was now waist-high in saw grass, unable to see any of his companions. He had spotted a floating piece of wood and grabbed it. It was half of a wooden oar.

Just then the head of a giant alligator broke the surface. With its great jaws open and ready to snap, it was lunging right at Joe!

3 Man-eater

Joe held out the half-oar, hoping it would keep the alligator at bay long enough for him to get to safety. The alligator jerked its head to the side and snapped the wood into bits.

Joe stumbled as he tried to run through the thick saw grass. He made it to shore seconds ahead of the alligator. He shuddered as the alligator's cloudy white eye seemed to look at him before it disappeared in the murky water of the swamp.

"Over here!" Frank shouted as he tramped down the shoreline toward his brother. Dusty, Chet, and Homer were a few steps behind him.

"Are you okay, Joe?" Chet asked.

"I'm not alligator chow, if that's what you mean," Joe replied.

"This is Homer Janes, the camp caretaker," Dusty said. "He's also my steer-roping partner."

"Call me Homer," the man insisted. "If you ask me, Weird Reuben had something to do with that big alligator coming after us. He has magic power over swamp creatures."

"Oh, quit it, Homer!" Dusty exclaimed, swatting him with the brim of his hat.

"Who's Weird Reuben?" Joe asked. Frank filled him in on Tallwalker's grandson and how they had spotted him on Twin Cypress Key.

"What happened here?" A blond man with a mustache and sky blue eyes called from the direction of the fishing camp, followed by three other men and a young woman.

"An alligator attacked us, Mr. Furman!" Homer blustered. "It was as long as two canoes strung nose to nose. Me and that boy were nearly eaten alive!"

Frank saw Furman walk to the water's edge. "Here's your problem," Furman said, carefully pulling back an armful of saw grass to reveal a mound of dead plants and leaves.

"An alligator mound!" Frank exclaimed, recognizing it from a picture he had seen in his book.

"It was just a mother alligator protecting her eggs," Furman explained.

"That's strange," Dusty said. "Alligators don't usually lay eggs this close to the bay. The water's too salty. They like it farther back in the swamp, away from people and boat traffic."

16

"Usually," Furman remarked. "But the fact is, this alligator seems to have made this key into her nursery."

"Could be a man-eater, Dusty," Homer warned. "If it's lost its fear of humans, it needs to be hunted down and killed."

"We'll attend to this problem later," Dusty said. "It's nearly noon, and we have to be at the rodeo by two o'clock."

The boys changed into dry clothes, ate a quick lunch of fresh trout and grits, and boarded Dusty's rectangular, flat-bottomed pontoon boat, which ferried his guests from the fishing camp to the mainland.

On the way, the Hardys met the other guests who were staying at the camp for the rodeo. Billy and Roy Biggs were a calf-roping team, Trent Furman was a wild-bull rider, and Ashley Walton was a bronco buster.

When they reached the trading post, Dusty and the others got into the back of Tallwalker's pickup truck and took off for the rodeo grounds.

"Have a good ride!" Dusty shouted as the pickup pulled out of the parking lot, kicking up a cloud of dust.

Chet suggested that he and the Hardys draw straws to see who got stuck riding the mule. A minute later, Chet pulled himself up onto the back of Old Caloosa.

Stonewall, Paint Can, and Old Caloosa were well trained, and they barely reacted to the cars, trucks, and horse trailers speeding by them on the two-lane highway, all headed for the Swampland Rodeo.

As the boys road horseback along the narrow shoulder of the highway, Chet lassoed every road sign they passed.

"Am I a dead-eye roper or what?" Chet grinned as he dismounted to remove the noose from a sign for the sixth time.

Joe shifted in his saddle. "Chet, if you don't stop that, we're going to miss the first day of competition completely."

Chet nodded and kept his rope coiled for the rest of the journey.

When the boys met up with Dusty and Homer at the rodeo, Dusty gave them a quick tour. He pointed out that the rodeo grounds were actually a section of a cattle ranch owned by a millionaire named Melvin Deeter.

Every year, Dusty told his companions, truck-loads of equipment and livestock were brought in for the rodeo. "They set up grandstands around the main rodeo ring and pitch that giant tent beside it."

"What's in the tent?" Joe asked.

"Farm exhibits, registration tables, concession stands, you name it," Dusty boasted. "We got us a chili cook-off, a livestock auction, not to mention three days of bronco busting and wild-bull riding. It's like a big old carnival!"

"What are those outer buildings beyond the corral?" Frank asked Homer.

"That's the barn, and the other is the bunkhouse where the rodeo riders keep their gear," Homer explained. "At the other end of the parking lot are the trailers where the judges and the rodeo clowns stay."

Walking into the main tent, the group joined the line to register Dusty and Homer for the competition. Joe looked over the sea of cowboys and spectators. "Where do most of the contestants come from?" he asked.

"A lot of them are locals from Frog's Peninsula," Dusty explained. "The rest of the competitors come from the rodeo circuit. They travel all over the country from one rodeo to the next."

"I'm only ten dollars short, Mr. Deeter," a tall, thin teenager at the front of the line shouted to a white-haired man with long sideburns.

"I'm sorry, young man," Deeter said. "If you come up with the ten dollars before tomorrow night's bull-riding competition, I'll let you compete. For now, you'll have to settle for the bronco busting tonight."

"Oh, okay," the teenager said with a sigh. He stood flipping a coin, while Mr. Deeter signed him up and handed him his official number. As the teenager turned, he caught Joe looking at him.

"What are you looking at?" he asked, facing Joe squarely.

"Nothing," Joe replied, sizing the teen up and deciding not to fight for no reason.

"Well, I'll give you guys something to see tonight," the teen boasted. "I'm going to win the bronco-riding competition."

As the teenager flipped his coin again, Joe caught a flash of gold. What is a guy who's ten dollars short doing with a gold coin? Joe wondered to himself.

"The name is Randy Stevens. You can look for my name at the top of the board," the teenager said, sticking his chin in the air. "'Cause I'm going to win."

Frank saw that Randy had attracted the attention of Trent Furman, who had been watching the scene from a nearby souvenir stand.

"That's some mighty big talk for a boy your age," Furman said, stepping over to Randy.

"I'm not a boy, mister," Randy shot back. "Who exactly are you?"

"The name's Trent Furman, I'm a bronco buster myself. Did I see you at the rodeo last year in Fargo, North Dakota?"

"Uh . . ." Randy suddenly seemed less confident.

"I won first place," Furman went on, smiling. "If you're half as good as you claim to be, I know someone who might sponsor you. He'll put up the cash for you to compete, in return for a cut of the prize money you win," Furman said.

"Well, I'm a rider worth sponsoring," Randy said, his confidence back.

"Let's go find this guy," Furman suggested.

"Aren't you going to register yourself?" Homer asked Furman.

"I'll do that later," Furman replied, putting a hand on Randy's shoulder and leading him away.

"That kid is too big for his britches," Dusty remarked, as he stepped up to the registration table.

"You'd better get moving," Deeter told Dusty as he handed him his official competition number. "Your bronco-riding competition starts in fifteen minutes."

"I'll see you all later," Dusty shouted over his shoulder as he headed out of the tent.

"Good luck!" Joe called after him.

"I'm thirsty," Frank said. "Who wants something to drink?"

"Whatever they have, I'll take a large," Chet replied.

"We'll meet you in the seats," Joe called as he and Chet started off toward the grandstands.

At the concession stand, Frank struck up a conversation with a couple of rodeo contestants in line in front of him. There was still a buzz about how the bank robbers had probably drowned in Florida Bay during the sudden winter storm.

By the time Frank reached the counter, he had gotten an invitation for him, Joe, and Chet to attend a barbecue behind the main tent that evening after the competition.

Frank was carrying three large lemonades toward the grandstands when he spotted the guests from the fishing camp engaged in an intense-looking discussion.

"Well, Billy and I like roughing it in the wilderness," Roy Biggs was saying, "but an alligator-infested island may be a little *too* rough."

"I'm with them," Furman added.

"I can take care of that for you," came a deep voice from behind them. Frank saw a familiar-looking man with a red beard step forward. "The name is Zack Platt. I've been handling alligators my whole life." Platt held up his right hand, and Frank saw he was missing his pinkie and part of his ring finger. "If you give me two nights and fifty dollars I'll get rid of your alligator problem," Platt said.

"It's illegal to kill alligators without a special license," Billy Biggs warned.

"I didn't say I was going to kill the alligator," Platt snapped back. "I'll trap it and relocate it to another part of the swamp."

"For fifty dollars, what do we have to lose?" Furman suggested to his fellow guests as he pulled out his wallet. "In fact, I'll pay for it."

"I have only one request," Platt said. "I work at night, and I can't have any of you folks snooping around, scaring off my quarry. Starting at midnight, everyone needs to keep clear of Gator Swamp."

As the others nodded eagerly to one another, Frank continued to the main rodeo ring and joined Chet and Joe in the grandstands. "Hey, Joe, you remember the man with the red beard you saw at the trading post? I think Furman just hired him to trap our giant alligator."

"He's an alligator trapper?" Joe asked. "I thought he was a snorkeler."

Frank nodded. "I guess he could be both. But didn't you say he was headed for Key West?"

Just then the gate opened, releasing the first bronco and its rider from the chute and into the ring.

"It's Randy Stevens!" Chet shouted.

Randy's body snapped back and forth like a whip as the horse beneath him bucked, kicking up its back legs. But the teenager held tight until the qualifying buzzer sounded.

Randy flew off the horse's back, landing with a soft thud on the thick plowed dirt of the ring. Two men dressed in baggy overalls and wearing clown makeup waved their hands frantically, getting the horse's attention. Then they quickly moved in, grabbed the reins, and got the bronco under control before taking it back to its holding pen.

"Hey, Chet, if you can't rope steers, maybe you can be one of those guys," Joe joked.

"Don't knock it," Chet replied. "Rodeo clowns

only look funny. It's a tough job—tough and dangerous."

Randy got up and bowed to the crowd, tipping his hat—a white hat with an orange-and-black feather in the band, Joe noticed.

"Hey!" he shouted. "Randy must have been the guy with Platt in the boat. I couldn't see his face, but he was wearing that exact same hat." He furrowed his brow. "I didn't see Randy wearing it when we met him in line a while ago."

"Me, either," Frank agreed. "Guess he put it on just before the competition."

"Dusty is next!" Chet exclaimed.

Dusty sat in the chute, high on a black horse named Nightmare. The gate opened, and Nightmare came out kicking, spinning in circles, trying to unseat his rider. But Dusty held on firmly to the reins and qualified easily. He whooped and hollered the whole time as if he were a kid on a roller coaster. As Dusty dismounted, he got a big round of applause. He was obviously a local favorite.

"And now Reuben Tallwalker, riding Volcano," Mr. Deeter announced over the public-address system. The crowd quieted instantly.

"Reuben Tallwalker? Isn't that the guy you saw watching you from Twin Cypress Key?" Joe asked.

The gate sprang open, and Volcano raced forward, kicking his back hooves high in the air. It seemed impossible that anyone could hang on, but Reuben rode the bucking horse easily. He jumped

24

gracefully to the ground and landed on his two feet directly in front of the Hardys and Chet.

Reuben stared at the three boys with his cold dark eyes. As the applause died out, he jumped up on the fence and spoke to the Hardys in an angry whisper: "Stay out of Gator Swamp or else."

With that, Reuben made a violent slashing motion across his throat and strode away.

4 Trouble at the Rodeo

"Wait!" Joe shouted. But Reuben ignored him and kept moving, slipping through a gate on the opposite side of the ring.

"What was that all about?" Chet asked.

"I don't know, but we're about to find out," Frank replied as he and Joe bolted for the spectators' exit.

When they came out on the far side, Reuben was nowhere in sight. Joe spotted a rodeo clown in a red ten-gallon hat leading Nightmare toward the great barn where the animals were kept.

"Did you see a guy with long black hair and a brightly colored, striped woven jacket?" Joe asked. The clown pointed toward a field behind the barn.

"There he is," Frank said, seeing a figure springing through the tall grass toward a heavily wooded area in the distance.

"He's headed for the swamp. I wouldn't follow him if I were you," the clown warned.

"Why not?" Joe replied as he watched Reuben disappear into the woods beyond the field.

"Because Reuben Tallwalker knows every inch of that swamp. He knows about the snakes and alligator holes and quicksand," the clown explained. "You'd last about five minutes in there."

"He's right, Joe," Frank agreed. "It'll be dark soon. We'd never find him."

"How do you know so much about Reuben Tallwalker?" Joe asked the rodeo clown.

"I know a lot about everyone in these parts—I've lived here all my life. The name's Barney Quick." Just then Nightmare reared up and whinnied, growing restless. "Excuse me, I have to get him put up for the night," Quick said, tipping his hat as he led Nightmare into the barn.

"Something's going on in Gator Swamp," Frank said to Joe and Chet.

"What do you mean?" Joe asked.

Frank told Joe and Chet about Zack Platt's promise to capture the giant reptile only if everyone stayed out of the swamp for the next two nights. "I'm going to try to find out something about Zack Platt," he finished. "Joe, you and Chet see if you can find out anything more about Randy and his connection to Platt."

"I have one burning question," Chet remarked. "Can we stop by the concession stand on the way?"

Frank spent the next hour striking up conversations with strangers, asking each if they knew anything about Zack Platt. None of the locals from Frog's Peninsula knew Platt, nor did any of the rodeo riders from the circuit.

Meanwhile, Chet and Joe searched the grandstands, then the main tent, and found Randy at the board where the results of the bronco-riding competition were posted.

"Hey, Randy," Joe said, trying to sound as friendly as he could.

Randy looked at Joe and Chet. "Oh, hi."

"How did you do?" Chet asked.

"Lousy," Randy muttered.

Joe studied the board. Dusty Cole had edged out Reuben Tallwalker for top honors. Randy had come in twelfth. "You stayed on until the buzzer," Joe said.

"That's only part of it. You're also judged on the difficulty of your horse and the quality of your ride," Randy explained.

"All they have to do is give you a tougher horse next time," Chet said.

"Yeah, that's right," Randy said, smiling.

"There you are!" Dusty called as he hurried over. "We're heading back to the trading post now."

"There's a barbecue for the younger crowd," Joe explained. "We thought we'd hang out awhile."

"I wish you could," Dusty replied. "But our guests are tired, and if you don't go back to the fishing camp with us on the pontoon boat, you'll be stranded."

"I could take them back," Randy offered. "My johnboat is docked at the trading post. If you're talking about Cole's Fishing Camp, it's on my way."

"Where's home?" Dusty asked.

"Frog's Peninsula," Randy replied.

"And you took a boat all the way across Gator Swamp to the trading post?" Dusty asked, puzzled. "You could have walked to the rodeo from Frog's Peninsula in half the time."

After a slight pause, Randy replied, "I like the scenic route."

Dusty gave Randy a suspicious look. Joe could see Randy growing nervous, and he didn't want to lose the chance to question him further. "Thanks, Randy. Hitching a ride back with you is a great idea."

"Be back at the camp by midnight," Dusty called as he headed for the parking lot. "You all promised Platt you'd stay out of the swamp after that."

"I'm going to catch a quick shower in the bunkhouse," Randy said. "I'll see you at the barbecue."

After Randy was gone, Chet turned to Joe. "I thought you were going to ask Randy what he was doing with Zack Platt?"

"I am," Joe replied, "but he won't open up if he's suspicious of us right off the bat."

Chet nodded. "First," Joe added, "I want to see what Frank's found out." Joe and Chet caught up with Frank by the bull pen, where he was talking with a couple of the rodeo cowhands.

"I found out that no one here knows a thing about Zack Platt," Frank said.

Joe filled Frank in on Randy's odd behavior. "I think Randy and Mr. Platt are doing something illegal in Gator Swamp," Joe concluded.

"Maybe they're poaching alligators," Frank offered. "They could be hunting them without a license and selling the hides on the black market."

Joe scratched his chin thoughtfully. "We might have to go into the swamp to find the answers."

"Swamps are scary places," Chet said. "I'd rather be tracking cold-blooded kidnappers in Bayport."

"Relax, Chet," Joe assured his friend. "For now all you have to do is eat barbecue."

"Of barbecue," Chet said with a smile, "I am fearless."

Behind the main tent, a group of young men and women were sitting around a blazing campfire. Rodeo workers were stringing white lights up on poles surrounding the area. Two huge barbecue grills had been set up nearby, and the boys could smell the aroma of spareribs cooking over the hot coals.

Deputy Miles, who was out of uniform and in a white blouse, blue jeans, and cowboy boots, was talking with Mr. Deeter. She waved to the Hardys and Chet as they approached.

Frank spotted Randy standing with some girls near the campfire, flipping his gold coin. "I'm not afraid of any wild bull," Randy boasted. "Watch me tomorrow. I'll be riding Storm Cloud."

"So Mr. Furman found you a sponsor," Frank said as he approached Randy.

"Yes, he did," Randy replied.

"Is that a good-luck charm or something?" Frank asked, nodding to the gold coin.

"Huh? Yeah, a good-luck charm," Randy replied, closing his hand on the coin so that Frank couldn't see it.

A tall balding man with black-rimmed glasses stepped from the shadows into the light of the campfire. "Better put that away before you lose it."

Randy pocketed his coin. "This is my sponsor, Mr. Salty Hubbard."

As Frank shook his rough bony hand, Hubbard added in a loud voice, "I'm a fisherman by trade. I just dabble in this rodeo stuff for fun. Are you boys friends of Randy?"

"Actually, we just met today," Frank replied.

"Is that right?" Hubbard replied. "So you don't know him any better than I do."

"No, sir," Joe replied. "Do you often sponsor riders you don't know?"

Hubbard laughed off Joe's question. "No. I just had a hunch about Randy."

"I think what my brother meant was, Randy's so young," Frank said. "We figured a sponsor looks for someone with more experience."

"I'm plenty old," Randy said hotly. "Eighteen. And so what if this is my first rodeo?"

Powerful hands were suddenly placed on Frank's and Joe's shoulders. "Shouldn't you two be home in bed by now?" The strong hands belonged to Zack Platt.

"Hello, Mr. Platt," Frank said, poking Joe with his elbow. "This is the alligator trapper I told you about. This is my brother, Joe."

Joe shook hands with Platt, giving Frank a quick look and nod indicating that this was, in fact, the man Joe had seen at the trading post that morning. "I thought you were headed for Key West," Joe said to Platt.

Platt's eyes narrowed. "Change in plans."

"And I guess you already know Randy Stevens," Joe gestured to Randy.

"No, I don't," Platt replied. "Howdy."

Joe furrowed his eyebrows, looking confused.

"Hey, there!" Randy greeted Platt, shaking hands. Joe caught Randy eyeing Platt's missing fingers as if he had never noticed them before. "Oh. Sorry, Mr. Platt, I didn't mean to . . ." The embarrassed teenager let his voice trail off.

Platt, seeming not to notice, turned his attention

to Frank. "I'm from Clewiston, a little town on Lake Okeechobee. I'm here because I have a friend competing in the rodeo. And I'm going after that alligator because I need the fifty dollars." Platt tightened his grip on the boys' shoulders. "If you have any more questions about me, I suggest you ask them to my face."

Platt released his grip, giving Frank and Joe a little shove, and walked off. Joe was ready to go after him, but Frank held him back.

"What was that all about?" Hubbard asked.

"Beats me," Joe said.

The fiddle player, who was using the back of a flatbed truck for a stage, was joined by a banjo player and bass player. "It's square-dancing time!" he called.

"Ladies' choice! Choose your partners!" the fiddle player shouted.

Before the boys could speak privately, two girls asked them to dance.

Frank saw that the lighted area was the dance floor. As more than twenty young people gathered, the fiddle player divided them into odd and even couples, then began calling the square dance. "Let's make one big circle, going left!"

"Randy acted as if he didn't know Mr. Platt," Joe said to Frank as they formed a circle with the rest of the group and began moving to the left. "Especially when he noticed Platt's missing fingers," he added.

"That was probably just an act so that no one would connect them to each other," Frank said.

"Odd couple pair off with the couple to your left," the fiddle player called, and Frank and his partner had to leave Joe and his partner and move on.

Joe was joined by Randy and his partner. "Now, you foursomes circle right," the fiddler called.

Randy was directly across from Joe in their circle of four. "Zack Platt sure seemed angry about something tonight, didn't he," Joe said, watching Randy's face closely.

"What are you talking about?" Randy replied.

"Put your right hands over," the fiddle player called. Randy thrust his hand out toward Joe, who flinched before realizing it was part of the square dance. Joe saw that the two girls had reached across the circle to grab each other's hand, and so he did the same.

"And now left hands back," the fiddler called, and everyone turned and circled in the opposite direction.

Joe decided to shock Randy into an honest response. "What's out in Gator Swamp that you're trying to hide?"

"Swing your partner and odd couples move on!" the fiddle player called. But Joe's last question had clearly taken Randy by surprise, and he didn't move.

"Hey, you're supposed to move on," Deputy

Miles said to Randy as she grabbed Joe's hand. "Well, if it isn't the teenage detective," she added with a friendly smile. Randy started to back away, looking scared.

"Dig for the oyster!" the fiddler called, and Joe's partner pulled him beneath the arched arms of Deputy Miles and her partner. Joe spun around, catching a glimpse of Randy on the opposite side of the campfire, running full speed into the darkness.

"He's getting away!" Joe shouted to Frank, who was now on the opposite side of the dance floor.

"Come on, Chet!" Frank called to his friend, who was sitting on a barrel, holding a slab of ribs.

Joe saw that there was a crowd of people to each side of the fire pit, so he took the most direct route.

Frank caught sight of Joe running full speed toward the blazing fire pit. "Don't, Joe! You'll never make it!"

It was too late. Joe stepped on the low wall of the fire pit and leaped.

5 No Way Home

Joe was in midair before he realized he might have made a dumb move. He could feel the intense heat on his legs and feet, but he soared through the flames so quickly that it didn't burn him.

He hit the other side of the eight-foot pit running and would have caught Randy if he hadn't tripped on someone's boot.

"I'm sorry," Salty Hubbard said, pulling Joe up off the ground. "Are you okay?" Joe didn't respond as his eyes scanned the area for Randy. Had Salty tripped him on purpose, Joe wondered, or was it just an accident?

Beyond the light of the fire, the night was pitch-black. Fifty yards ahead, Joe saw a car screech to a halt to avoid hitting a figure in the road. In the headlights, Joe spotted Randy in his telltale white hat as the teenager quickly opened the passenger door and climbed in.

The car drove on just as Frank ran up. "What happened?"

"When Deputy Miles let on that I was an amateur detective, Randy took off like a shot," Joe said.

Chet caught up to his friends. "What's going on?"

"Randy hitched a ride with someone and got away," Joe replied.

"There goes our ride," Chet joked.

"Come on," Frank said. "We'd better tell Deputy Miles what we've found out."

The boys quickly told Deputy Miles about everything that had happened since the afternoon.

"It all seems very odd," Deputy Miles said. "I don't know Zack Platt or Randy Stevens, but I'll check with headquarters. And I definitely want to question Reuben about his threatening you. Finding him is the problem."

"If he's going to compete in the bull riding, he'll have to be here tomorrow night," Frank pointed out.

"Right," Deputy Miles said. "I'll meet you boys tomorrow evening at five o'clock, right here by the fire pit."

"By the way, Deputy Miles, did you ever find the robbers' getaway boat on Frog's Peninsula?" Frank asked.

Deputy Miles frowned. "Not yet. Florida Bay is huge, and with that storm—"

"The loot probably wasn't on board the sunken airboat." Joe finished the sentence for her.

"We haven't even found the robbers' bodies. The storm probably swept them out to sea," Deputy Miles explained.

"And the money could be floating somewhere in the Caribbean by now," Frank said.

"No. That's one thing we don't have to worry about," Deputy Miles said.

"What do you mean?" Frank asked.

"I mean this particular loot wouldn't float," Deputy Miles replied. Before Frank could ask her to explain, she checked her watch and said, "Well, looks like the night's activities are winding down. Good night, boys. And don't worry. The Coast Guard has all kinds of high-tech equipment. They'll recover the bodies and the money."

After Deputy Miles left, Chet said, "We'd better get our horses."

As they approached the barn, Barney Quick was leading out Stonewall, Paint Can, and Old Caloosa.

"Here're your two horses and your, uh, mule," Quick said with a grin. "I was beginning to think you boys had left without them."

"Well," Chet said with a sigh as he pulled himself up onto Old Caloosa's back, "we've got ourselves another mystery."

"I've got an even bigger mystery we have to solve,

Joe said. "How are we going to get across Gator Swamp tonight?"

The highway was empty. The road was visible only because of the light of the half-moon reflecting off it. The boys rode in silence for a while. Joe and Frank were quiet because their minds were deep in thought. Chet was quiet because he was concentrating on staying on Old Caloosa.

"What if Zack Platt and Randy Stevens found something in Gator Swamp that they don't want anyone else to know about?" Frank ventured.

"Like that stolen loot?" Chet asked. "But where does Reuben Tallwalker fit in?"

Frank shrugged. "Deputy Miles said something odd about the money. She said that this particular loot wouldn't float."

"Another weird thing," Joe said, "was the way Randy and Mr. Platt acted when they met. I really don't think they knew each other."

"But if Randy doesn't know Mr. Platt, how could you have seen them together at the trading post this morning?" Frank pointed out.

"Maybe it wasn't Randy who was wearing the white hat this morning," Joe offered. "It's possible someone else could have the same one as Randy."

"Good point. Or maybe Randy and Mr. Platt are just both good liars," Frank suggested.

"If they were lying, they're the *best* liars we've ever run across," Joe concluded.

Suddenly Joe heard a twig snap. The Hardys reined in their horses and looked toward the thick undergrowth beside the road.

Without a word, Frank signaled for Joe and Chet to dismount. He pointed to himself and toward the woods in front of them. Then he pointed to Joe and toward the woods behind them.

Joe nodded, understanding that they were going to come at the sound they had heard from opposite directions.

"Stay with the horses," Joe whispered to Chet as he headed into the thick underbrush. Joe felt his foot slip into something soft and wet. Looking down, he discovered that he was standing in a foot of water and muck. He wondered if there was solid ground anywhere in the Everglades.

Headed in the other direction, Frank was finding the going just as tough. He was also slogging through mud and, on top of that, seemed to have attracted a large family of mosquitoes. He couldn't even see them to shoo them away. He only knew they were there because he felt them biting him.

Finally Frank was able to make something out in the darkness—something white, hanging on a branch, catching the moonlight.

Frank stretched out his hand, but just as he grabbed the white object, someone jumped him from behind. Frank and his assailant tumbled forward into the muck.

On the road, Chet could hear branches shaking

and the sound of a scuffle. "Frank? Joe! Are you okay? What did you find?" Chet shouted.

There was a pause. "We found each other," Frank's voice came from the brush. Joe and Frank emerged wet and muddy, looking a bit annoyed with each other.

It was too dark for Frank to tell exactly what he had grabbed off the branch. He could tell it was a piece of cloth. "It could be a handkerchief or a torn patch off a shirt," he told the others.

The three boys agreed that their best bet was to get to the trading post as soon as possible. If someone wanted to follow them through the muck and mosquitoes beside the road, they were welcome to do so.

It was nearly midnight when they arrived at the trading post. It was closed, and Angus Tallwalker had gone home. He had left the door to the stable open, though, so the boys put their mounts into their stalls. The only light came from the soda machine by the stable door, and Frank held the piece of white cloth in front of it.

"It's a rodeo rider's number!" Joe exclaimed.

"Number forty-five. Wasn't that Reuben's number?" Frank asked.

Joe snapped his fingers. "Yes. That means Reuben didn't run off. He must have circled around and waited for us outside the rodeo so he could follow us."

"Reuben warned us not to go into Gator Swamp,"

Frank recalled. "Maybe he was making sure we didn't."

"Well, I hate to disappoint him," Chet remarked, "but that's the only way home."

"I don't think Angus Tallwalker would mind if we borrowed a boat," Frank suggested.

Unfortunately, they discovered that all the boats were chained to the dock for the night. Frank tried to pick the lock with the penknife that he always kept handy, but the locks were too strong and the lighting was too dim.

"Sorry, guys," Frank said, closing the penknife.

"Wait a second," Chet said, snapping his fingers. "I just remembered something. Follow me."

The Hardys followed their friend around the back of the trading post and into Angus Tallwalker's junkyard. "There's our ride home," Chet said, pointing to an odd-looking watercraft.

Joe frowned. "It looks like a cross between an aquatic bicycle and a Stone Age jet-ski."

"It's a pedal boat! We used to rent them at a place I went to as a little kid," Chet explained.

"Where's the engine?" Frank asked.

"There is no engine," Chet replied. "You pedal it with your feet."

"It'll take us hours to get back to the fishing camp," Joe complained.

"I'm not even sure it's seaworthy," Frank added.

"Who knows," Chet remarked. "But do we have a choice?"

"You're right, Chet," Frank said. "We should be grateful you remembered it was here."

Dragging the pedal boat down to the dock, they set it in the water and climbed aboard. Chet took the only seat, pumping the pedals with his feet, while the Hardys kneeled down, trying to keep the tiny craft balanced.

They churned through the water at about one mile per hour.

"In this tub, we'll never get to the fishing camp before the midnight curfew," Joe said.

"What better excuse to nose around Gator Swamp when we're not supposed to?" Frank replied, smiling.

The boys took turns pedaling. Even so, after nearly an hour, they were all exhausted.

"Hey, Joe," Chet said, "you stopped pedaling."

"My calves are cramping," Joe moaned.

"I think we're almost there," Frank assured him.

Joe nodded, "No pain, no gain." He took a deep breath and started pedaling again.

"Wait!" Chet said suddenly. "Look over there!"

Off the starboard side of the craft, the shadowy silhouette of an island marked by two trees rose out of the swamp. Just in front of it, the boys saw an eerie light, moving slowly back and forth, like a single wandering eye.

"Maybe it's Zack Platt in his airboat," Joe said.

"There's no boat," Chet shot back. "That light is beneath the water."

"Listen!" Joe said in a loud whisper. "Whatever it is, it doesn't sound human." They heard the faint sound of raspy gurgling breathing and a muffled humming noise.

Joe got the boat as close as he could. They were only forty yards from the light when the light went out. The only illumination now was the half-moon reflecting off the surface of the water.

"Bubbles!" Chet said in a choked voice. Sure enough, Frank and Joe could see a path of small bubbles rising to the surface and headed in their direction.

"What do you think it is?" Joe asked.

"Whatever it is," Frank replied, "it's going right underneath our boat."

"It's the alligator!" Chet shouted.

Suddenly something struck the bottom of the boat with tremendous force, and the boys felt the craft begin to tip over.

6 Stranded

"Jump!" Joe shouted.

When the pedal boat flipped, the three boys were sent flying into the swamp.

"Swim for it!" Frank ordered, doing his best freestyle toward the two trees on the nearby island.

Joe kicked his legs violently behind him, hoping to drive away the alligator if it was pursuing them.

Suddenly Joe's knee hit something. Mud. The water was only a few feet deep. Joe rose up and slogged through the water and onto the shore. He gave Chet and Frank a hand, and all three quickly climbed into the limbs of one of the tall trees. There was no sign of the alligator or the mysterious light.

"What do we do now?" Chet asked.

"We'd better stay here until daybreak. Then we can figure out where we are," Joe replied.

The boys tried to make themselves comfortable in the tree. Frank, Joe, and Chet were beyond tired. Despite the occasional mosquito bite or cry of a passing egret, they slept through the rest of the night.

Joe woke up briefly, thinking that he felt something cold on his forehead. But everyone else was asleep. Joe figured he must have been dreaming and fell quickly back to sleep.

The next time Joe's eyes opened, it was morning and something was poking him in the ribs. Joe was relieved to see it was Homer, standing in the pontoon boat beside the shore, prodding Joe up in the tree with the end of a cane fishing pole.

"What in the world happened to you three?" Homer asked. "We've been worried as a fat hen in a fox's den."

"Homer!" Chet said, waking up. "Boy, are we glad to see you. How did you find us?"

"It wasn't too hard," Homer replied, pointing across the water with his pole. No more than a hundred yards away was an island, dotted with cabins on stilts.

"The fishing camp?" Joe exclaimed. "We're on Twin Cypress Key."

"Wow, Frank," Chet said, "you really did know where you were going."

"What's the joke?" Homer asked. "Who knows the Seminole language?"

The boys exchanged confused looks. Then Frank said, "Joe, your forehead!"

Joe's forehead had been painted with mud. "Yours, too," Joe replied. Frank also had something written in mud on his forehead, and so did Chet. The boys climbed down from the limbs of the tree.

"Did you say these were Seminole words?" Frank asked.

"Yep," Homer replied, pointing first to Frank. "Yours says 'Last,' Joe's says 'Your,' and Chet's says 'Warning.'"

"Last your . . ." Joe said, before it hit him. "Your last warning."

"Or, rather, our last warning," Frank said, giving Joe a knowing look. "From none other than Reuben Tallwalker, no doubt."

"Couldn't be anyone else," Homer agreed.

"How could he climb that tree and do this without waking us up?" Chet asked as he dipped his hand into the water and began rubbing off the mud.

"Folks say he can move in, out, and around as quietly as snowflakes falling," Homer replied in a warning tone.

"We were dead tired, too, don't forget," Frank noted. "I would have slept through a car alarm."

There was the sound of an approaching airplane.

47

Homer waved as Dusty's hydroplane buzzed over them.

"Dusty's been out looking for you since dawn," Homer told them, starting up the engine of his boat. "We'd better tell him you're okay."

Back in their cabin, the boys showered and put on dry clothes. "Based on the number of bites," Chet said, looking at the raised red bumps on his arms and face, "I was the mosquitoes' midnight snack."

Chet was coating the bites with lotion to stop the itching when Dusty popped his head through the door. "Boy, am I glad to see you safe and sound!"

Frank and Joe filled Dusty in on everything, beginning with Randy Stevens running off and leaving them at the rodeo when he found out they were detectives.

"Don't forget the mysterious light in the swamp," Chet added.

"That could have been the moon reflecting off the surface," Dusty said. "The thing that has me confused is these alligator attacks. You weren't near her clutch of eggs. Why would that big mama alligator attack you for no reason?"

"Maybe it's Reuben's pet. Like an attack alligator," Chet suggested. Frank and Joe shared an amused look over their friend's joke.

"I have a friend who runs an alligator farm in Big Cypress Swamp," Dusty said. "He knows more about reptiles than the reptiles do. Maybe he can explain it."

"What about the rodeo? Aren't you competing tonight?" Joe asked, concerned.

"I'll be back in time," Dusty replied.

"Would you mind if I came along?" Frank asked.

"Not at all," Dusty said. "Maybe I'll even give you a chance to fly the hydroplane."

"Meanwhile, Chet and I will go back to the scene of the attack," Joe said. "Maybe we can figure out some details about what happened now that it's daylight."

"And why don't we rent our own boat from the trading post?" Chet suggested.

"Good idea," Joe remarked, rubbing the pedaling muscles in his calves. "I don't want to get stuck without wheels again."

Frank agreed and gave Chet and Joe some money toward the boat rental, then they all headed for the hydroplane.

As Frank and Dusty were boarding the hydroplane, Trent Furman came strolling down the dock, sipping a mug of coffee. "I heard you got into some alligator trouble again."

"Yes, sir," Chet replied, scratching his shoulder. "Mosquito trouble, too."

"That'll teach you boys to go into the swamp alone at night," Furman said sharply.

Frank gave Furman a probing look. Furman's

hard gaze turned to a warm smile. "Just kidding, boys. Hey, I'll bet Zack Platt will catch that big alligator tonight. Then it'll be safe for all of us."

"Where was Mr. Platt?" Joe asked. "We were stranded out there all night and didn't see him."

"I guess you just didn't cross paths," Furman said lightly. "Where are you going now?" he added, skillfully changing the subject.

"Big Cypress Swamp," Dusty replied.

"Sounds exciting. What's there?" Furman wondered.

"An alligator farm," Dusty replied.

Frank saw Furman's expression cloud for a moment before he recovered and smiled again. "Well," Furman said, "have a safe trip." He tipped his hat and returned to his cabin.

A minute later Dusty and Frank were airborne and flying north toward Big Cypress Swamp.

Joe and Chet headed for the lodge to try to find Homer. As they passed beneath Furman's window, Joe heard the crackle of a shortwave radio and Furman's voice. "They'll be there in less than an hour."

"Okay. We'll take care of it at this end," another voice replied over the radio. There was so much static that it distorted the other voice, and Joe had no chance of recognizing it.

"Ten-four," Furman's voice replied, then Joe heard him switch off the radio.

Joe and Chet found Homer in the main lodge,

tying his own fly fishing lures. Homer was planning to do some trout fishing, and he was a little grumpy about being asked to take Joe and Chet to the trading post instead.

Joe mentioned Furman's shortwave radio and the strange bit of conversation he had overheard.

"I know all about his radio. That's the only way to communicate with the outside world from here," Homer grumbled. "I have a shortwave radio, too, and I suppose that means *I'm* up to no good?"

Joe could see Homer was in no mood to discuss anything reasonably, so he said nothing more. Chet asked if their first stop could be at the scene of last night's accident. Homer grumbled, but said yes.

In daylight, Joe thought, the swamp didn't look at all menacing. He spotted the corner of the sunken pedal boat sticking out of the water. "I'll get it," he said to the others. Joe had worn swimming trunks under his clothes, pledging to keep at least one set of clothes dry for a whole day.

"You sure you want to go in that water?" Homer asked, worried. "The water's murky, and who knows what could be down there."

"If you two keep your eyes peeled, I should be all right," Joe replied as he took off his T-shirt.

With that, he slipped over the bow of the pontoon boat and into the water. He discovered he could just touch the muddy bottom on tiptoe. Finding the rudder, he began running his hand along the hull of the boat until he found a hole in the fiberglass.

Joe stretched, turning his chin up to keep his mouth above the surface. "There's a hole in the bottom of the boat."

"I could have told you that," Homer replied. "The alligator probably rammed it with its snout."

"Wait!" Joe said, excited. "There's something wedged in the hole. It's stuck in here pretty well."

Joe was happy he had been pumping iron all year. With his powerful arms, he was able to pry the object free. He handed it up to Chet, then pulled himself aboard the pontoon boat.

Chet and Homer were staring at the object, stunned. "There's your ghost," Joe said.

It was a heavy-duty waterproof flashlight. A sticker on the top of it read Property of the Swampland Trading Post.

7 A Missing Giant

The trading post was bustling with activity, as the people from the rodeo had the morning free before the contest resumed that afternoon. When Angus Tallwalker saw Joe and Chet, he scowled and turned away, making a point to help every other customer in the store before he even looked at them.

"We'd like to rent one of your airboats," Joe asked finally, when there was no one else in the store for Tallwalker to help.

"I don't have any to rent," Tallwalker responded, although Joe spotted the keys to two of the airboats still hanging on their hooks behind the counter.

"Is there something wrong, Mr. Tallwalker?" Joe pressed.

Tallwalker stared at him a moment. "How would you like it if I went to the cemetery in the town you're from and pitched a tent over your great-grandfather?"

Joe realized what Tallwalker meant. "So Reuben told you we got stranded on Twin Cypress Key?"

"Stranded?" Tallwalker said sarcastically. "Reuben told me you've been out there swimming and poking around."

"That's not true," Joe protested.

"That island was sacred to my grandfather. It is still important to me and my grandson," Tallwalker said angrily. "Last night you camped out in one of the cypress trees."

"Only because Reuben sank our pedal boat!" Chet countered.

Tallwalker looked confused. "Do you mean *my* old pedal boat from the junkyard?"

"Um, yeah," Chet replied, bowing his head, embarrassed. "Sorry."

"Reuben wouldn't do something like that," Tallwalker insisted.

"Then why did we find this stuck in the hull?" Joe said, setting the flashlight on the counter.

"What makes you think it's Reuben's?" Tallwalker asked.

Joe pointed to the label on top, but Tallwalker just shook his head. "That flashlight has been missing since yesterday. In fact, I haven't seen it since you were alone in here while Dusty and I were fetching your horses. Maybe you stole it."

"And maybe you're just protecting your grandson!" Joe snapped back.

There was a tense silence. Joe realized his temper had gotten the better of him. "I'm sorry, Mr. Tallwalker. It was stupid of me to accuse you."

"And I read people well enough to know you wouldn't steal from me," the older man replied, patting Joe's shoulder.

Chet was also apologetic. "I don't blame you for being upset, but we ended up sleeping in that tree because we had no other choice. Honest!"

Tallwalker rubbed his chin. "Maybe Reuben hasn't told me everything."

"Where is he now?" Joe asked.

"Early this morning he packed some gear. He said he would be camping out in Gator Swamp for the next few nights to keep the rodeo people away from Twin Cypress Key."

"I think a big part of this mystery could be cleared up if we could just talk to Reuben," Joe suggested.

Tallwalker paused, deciding whether or not to speak. "There's a chance you could find him. He usually camps in an abandoned poacher's shack at the east end of Gator Swamp."

"How are we going to get there?" Chet asked.

"I'm going to rent you a boat, of course." Tallwalker grinned.

Five minutes later Joe was in the skipper's perch of an airboat, getting instructions from Tallwalker on how to operate it.

Joe turned the ignition key, and the giant fan propeller spun into motion. The powerful breeze from the fan flattened the saw grass behind them. It was the loudest engine Joe had ever heard, and Chet had to cover his ears until he got used to it.

Tallwalker untied the bowline, and the boys cast off.

"Do you have the map to the poacher's shack?" Joe shouted. Chet held up the map Tallwalker had drawn for them. Joe gave the thumbs-up sign, and they headed for the east end of Gator Swamp.

Frank checked the control panels and gauges in the cockpit as Dusty brought the hydroplane in for a landing. By watching the speedometer and keeping track of the flying time, Frank figured they were about one hundred and twenty miles north of Gator Swamp.

Dusty set the hydroplane down on a small lake that bordered the Big Cypress Alligator Farm. Frank saw a young Native American man wave to them from a clearing on the shore. The man then pointed to the ground beneath him.

"I think that's where he wants us to park the plane," Frank suggested. "Or dock the plane, or whatever you do with one of these things."

Dusty smiled as he guided the hydroplane and

let it coast right up onto the grass on the shore. "Willow, you old snake lover, how are you!" Dusty shouted in his booming voice.

Frank could tell by the way the two men clapped each other on the back that they were close friends.

"I'm Steven Willow," the man said to Frank. "Welcome to Big Cypress Alligator Farm."

"I'm Frank Hardy," Frank replied, shaking the man's hand.

"We need to ask you some questions about alligator behavior," Dusty said.

"Sure. I've got a busy day today, so I hope you don't mind walking while we talk." Willow motioned them forward, and as they walked, Frank and Dusty told him about the strange attacks.

Frank thought the Big Cypress Alligator Farm looked a lot like a zoo. He saw a number of walled pits with various types and sizes of alligators, caimans, and crocodiles. There were also a dozen cages filled with snakes, iguanas, turtles, and other reptiles.

Frank heard a grunting sound from a distant corner of the farm. "What's that?"

"Baby alligators," Willow explained. "They grunt to let their mother know that they've hatched."

Willow stopped beside one of the pits. Frank looked into it and counted twenty-one alligators lying in the sun at the edge of a shallow moat filled with water. The alligators were so still that Frank thought they looked like stuffed replicas.

One rose up on its stumpy legs, walked to the edge of the moat, and slid into the water. Although none of them were nearly the size of the giant that attacked Joe, Frank felt a little nervous when Willow climbed down a ladder into the pit, armed with nothing but a six-foot-long wooden pole and a small bag.

First, Willow approached one of the alligators from behind. "They have a lousy field of vision," Willow explained. "Humphrey can't see me right now."

"Humphrey?" Frank wondered aloud.

"This screwball names all his alligators," Dusty replied. "To tell the truth, I don't know how he tells them apart."

Willow grabbed Humphrey by the tail and swiftly dragged him backward and away from the others. In an instant, Willow had dropped onto the alligator's back, grabbed its snout, and pulled its head up. Pulling a rope from his bag, he wrapped it around the alligator's snout, securing the jaws.

"All the alligator's muscles are for biting down," Willow explained. "Once the jaws are shut, I can keep them shut with my two fingers."

"You look like a calf roper." Dusty laughed.

"Tell me, Dusty, you ever heard of a calf biting off a man's fingers?" Willow joked.

The image of Zack Platt's missing fingers shot

through Frank's mind. "Did Humphrey bite off someone's fingers?" he asked Willow.

"Shh," Willow warned Frank as he rolled Humphrey over and, still sitting on top of him, began rubbing the smooth white underbelly. In a minute, he had put Humphrey to sleep.

"Tell me if any of the others try to sneak up on me," Willow said with a grin. Frank had to admire Willow's style. The man seemed fearless.

"Humphrey's sick," Willow explained, pulling a vial of medicine and a large syringe from his bag. "As you can see, he doesn't like taking his medicine." The reptile expert gave the alligator an injection, rolled him back over, untied his snout, then quickly climbed out of the pit.

"As for your alligator problem," Willow continued, wiping off his hands on a rag, "it sounds as if she was protecting her nest. My only guess is the alligator's usual breeding area is polluted or has dried up. Otherwise, she wouldn't want to lay her eggs on your island."

"What about the second attack on our pedal boat?" Frank asked. "We weren't near her nest."

Willow shrugged. "Could be she's sick or starving. Without checking the alligator myself firsthand, I can't give you one clear answer."

They were walking past another pit now, and curiosity made Frank take a look. He saw a sign that read Big Bertha, Largest Alligator in Florida. There appeared to be no alligator in the pit.

"Where's Big Bertha hiding?" Frank asked.

Willow frowned. "Strangest thing . . . I opened up two days ago and the pit was empty. Fifteen feet of alligator, gone. Her eggs were gone, too. The locks were still on the gates. I can't figure it out."

"Sounds like a lot of trouble. Who would take such a big risk to steal one alligator?" Dusty asked.

Willow shrugged. "Big Bertha was the meanest alligator I've ever seen. It would take an expert handler to get her out. Could have been someone from another alligator farm."

Frank's eyes widened, as he began connecting things in his mind. Zack Platt's missing fingers, a stolen alligator, the locks on the gates still intact. Things were falling into place.

Willow continued, "But they'll never get away with it. Bertha is easily identified."

"She has one white eye," Frank blurted.

Willow looked stunned. "Yes, she's blind in that eye. How did you know?"

"Did a man named Zack Platt ever work here?" Frank asked.

"Yeah, briefly," Willow replied. "I fired him last winter because I caught him stealing from the cash register."

"And Humphrey bit off two of his fingers?" Frank guessed.

Willow looked at Dusty. "Is Frank psychic?"

"No, he's just the smartest sleuth since Sherlock Holmes!" Dusty responded proudly.

"I think Zack Platt planted Big Bertha on your island to keep people away from that part of Gator Swamp," Frank said with excitement in his voice.

"Why?" Dusty asked.

"He's hunting for something, and I don't think it's alligators," Frank concluded.

"What is it, then?" Dusty demanded.

"A sunken treasure," Frank replied.

"From an old Spanish galleon?" Willow asked.

"No, from a bank vault in Miami," Frank replied. "But I don't want to make more accusations until I have some proof," he added. "Dusty, could you take me to Frog's Peninsula? I want to talk to Deputy Miles as soon as possible."

Willow escorted Dusty and Frank back to the shore of the lake and helped them slide the hydroplane off the grass and back into the water.

"Here's your chance," Dusty said, opening the door to the hydroplane and pointing to the pilot's seat. "Ready to try a takeoff?"

Frank was excited, but nervous. "Sure."

He climbed into the pilot's seat and quickly reviewed the controls and flying procedures with Dusty. He started the engine and taxied away from the dock and began his takeoff run. It felt more like he was water skiing than getting ready to lift off.

"Pull up on the controls," Dusty instructed. "A little more . . . a little more."

Frank felt the plane lift off the surface of the water. He aimed the nose of the plane for the tops of the trees bordering the lake. Frank gasped as the plane barely cleared the treetops, but Dusty just gave an excited holler.

Looking below, Frank spotted a white pickup truck parked at the side of the road leading to the alligator farm. A man was standing beside the truck, looking up at the hydroplane. It was a man in a white hat.

That was when Frank heard the hydroplane's engine sputter. The engine sputtered again and then cut off. The nose began to dip. The plane was going down!

8 Crash Landing!

"I'm taking over, good buddy!" Dusty shouted, grabbing the controls. "I've got to set her down as soon as possible."

Frank remained calm, scanning the ground for a makeshift landing area. "What about that big meadow?"

"That's saw grass. There's probably a few feet of water beneath it," Dusty said.

Dusty pulled back on the controls as far as he could, trying to get the nose of the plane to rise, but it was no use. The tips of the pontoons hit the saw grass at an awkward angle. The plane skipped off the shallow water like a flat stone.

Dusty took the split second he had to bring up the nose of the plane enough so it touched down squarely on the pontoons when it dropped back down again. The plane shuddered and shook as it tore through the saw grass and finally came to rest, tilting to one side.

"Are you okay?" Dusty asked.

"I think so," Frank replied.

"Now you know what it's like to ride a wild bull," Dusty said, winking.

"Next time there's an emergency, I'll be able to land it myself," Frank said.

Dusty and Frank climbed out of the plane. Considering what it had been through, the hydroplane didn't look too badly damaged. Frank took a look at the engine and quickly found the problem. "Someone severed the fuel line. We've been sabotaged!"

Frank and Dusty slogged through the saw grass until they finally reached a clearing and an unpaved road covered in broken seashells.

Frank heard a car approaching. It was a pickup truck but not a white one. It was older and painted dark green.

"Willow!" Dusty shouted, taking off his hat and waving it down.

Willow stopped the truck and jumped out. "I heard the airplane's engine sputter and die. I thought you were goners!"

"We would have been if Dusty wasn't such a good pilot," Frank replied. He told Willow about the white pickup truck and about the sabotaged fuel line.

"No one I know around here drives a white pickup," Willow replied.

"I didn't think so," Frank said. "It was Zack Platt's accomplice, Randy Stevens."

"The kid from the rodeo?" Dusty asked in disbelief.

"He was wearing the white hat," Frank replied.

"A white cowboy hat? That's not so unusual in these parts," Willow said with a chuckle.

"Not like this one. It has a black-and-orange feather," Frank said firmly. "Of course, I couldn't be sure about the feather from that distance," he added.

Dusty looked up at the sky. "Whoever or whatever, you boys must be sniffing pretty near the fox's den for them to risk sabotaging our aircraft."

"Listen, I know a fellow in Fort Myers. I can get him out here to fix the fuel hose this afternoon," Willow offered. "Meanwhile, you can borrow my pickup to get to Frog's Peninsula."

"Thanks," Dusty replied. "But we're so isolated out on Cole's Key, I need the hydroplane in case there's an emergency and I have to get help."

"How long will it take to get the plane fixed?" Frank asked.

Willow frowned. "You'll be stuck here at least five hours."

Dusty and Frank checked their watches and

exchanged worried looks. The wild-bull-riding competition was to start at seven, and it was already three o'clock.

"I'll tell you what," Willow said. "I'll fly the plane down to you myself tomorrow. Tonight, if I can."

"That's too much to ask, partner," Dusty replied. But Willow insisted, and five minutes later Dusty and Frank were in the pickup, rumbling down the dirt road that would connect them to the highway leading to Frog's Peninsula.

Back in Gator Swamp, Joe and Chet were making good time tracking down Reuben Tallwalker. The airboat could really move, skimming right through the algae and reeds in just a few inches of water.

"It should be down this next creek to the left!" Chet shouted.

Joe spotted the old wooden shack in the distance, at the edge of the creek. Its tin roof was rusty and sagging. The screens in the windows were torn. Inside, it looked dark and foreboding.

"Maybe we should hide the boat in the tall saw grass here and walk up through the woods so we're not seen," Chet suggested.

"Good idea," Joe said as he cut the motor. After securing the boat to a mangrove tree, Joe and Chet slipped quietly through the heavy growth beside the creek. To Joe's relief, the ground was relatively solid.

Joe motioned for Chet to stop. Through an opening between two mangroves, Joe had an excellent view of the shack. All was quiet and still, with no sign of Reuben Tallwalker.

"You stay here, Chet. I'm going inside," Joe instructed. "If anyone comes, give me some kind of signal."

Joe crawled on all fours to the back of the poacher's shack and peered through a window. It was pretty dark inside, but Joe could see that no one was home, so he climbed through the window.

Joe sniffed the air. It was damp and smelled of mildew. Flies buzzed in and out the window. There was a straw mattress on the floor and a jug of water, but not much else. Then Joe spotted a plastic bag in a corner.

Inside the bag, Joe found a snorkel and swim mask and some kind of portable mechanical device. Its small, square control box had a handle and dial on it. A four-foot-long metal pole protruding from the bottom of the control box had a small metal hoop at the end. Joe turned the dial, and the device hummed to life.

As he passed the device over the metal rim of the swim mask, it whirred loudly. "It's a metal detector," Joe said quietly. He remembered the whirring sound they had heard in the swamp the night before. He recalled another odd sound they had heard—the raspy breathing.

Joe placed his hand on the snorkel and smiled. It

wasn't a conjured spirit we saw in the swamp, it was a person snorkeling, he thought, searching for something underwater with a flashlight and a metal detector.

Joe's train of thought was broken by another strange sound. It took him a second to realize what it was: the call of a wood duck. Chet was warning him that someone was coming.

Through the screen of a front window, Joe could see that a canoe had been pulled up onto shore. He also saw Reuben Tallwalker walking toward the shack carrying a large heavy-bladed knife.

"A machete," Joe said under his breath. He knew he had only a second to act. Taking one giant step, he jumped through the back window of the shack.

Hitting the ground on his shoulder, he rolled down an embankment, coming to rest in a large puddle of water. Joe was soaking wet again, but at least he had escaped unnoticed.

He quietly circled around to the side of the shack where Chet was hiding.

"He's inside," Chet whispered. "Are you okay?"

Joe nodded. "I found a snorkel, a swim mask, and a metal detector. It probably wasn't an alligator we encountered in the swamp last night. I'm guessing it was Reuben, and he was using that equipment to search for something."

"What do you think he was searching for?" Chet asked. Joe shook his head.

The screen door of the poacher's shack creaked open. Reuben stepped out, holding the metal detector and snorkeling gear.

Joe and Chet ducked down behind some thick bushes, lying on their stomachs to avoid being spotted.

Reuben walked down beside his canoe and then, to Joe's surprise, hurled the metal detector into the middle of the creek. He hacked the snorkel and swim mask into bits with his machete.

Stepping into his canoe, the young Seminole paddled down the creek, around a bend, and out of sight.

Chet waited until the coast was clear before he spoke. "Why would he wreck all that stuff? Was he destroying evidence?"

"No," Joe replied. "He'd have to be pretty dumb to leave the remains right in front of a shack where he's known to stay." Joe paused. "I wish Frank were here. We could sure use his brainpower right now."

"He and Dusty should be back at the fishing camp by now," Chet said. "And we've got to get back there, too, before they leave for the rodeo."

When Chet and Joe returned to Cole's Fishing Camp, Homer rushed to greet them. He had a grim look on his face.

"I just overheard a local news flash on the shortwave," Homer said. "A small private plane made a crash landing in Big Cypress Swamp this morning. It was a hydroplane."

"Frank," Joe muttered.

"What happened?" Trent Furman asked, as he joined them on the dock.

"A crash landing in Big Cypress Swamp," Homer replied. "I think it might have been Dusty and Frank."

"Oh, no. That's terrible," Furman responded.

"Don't act innocent!" Joe shouted. "I heard you on the radio telling someone 'they'll be there in less than an hour.' And your accomplice said he would 'take care of it.'"

"Accomplice?" Furman smiled. "I was talking to a friend at the rodeo who has a buyer for a couple of my horses. I told my friend that 'they'—the horses—would be there in an hour."

"What friend?" Joe challenged.

"Simmer down, Joe. You have no right to go accusing one of the guests of such nonsense!" Homer scolded.

Billy Biggs stepped out of the lodge. "Homer," he called, "you've got someone trying to reach you on the shortwave radio. It's Dusty."

Joe, Chet, and Homer were in the lodge in no time flat. "Dusty! Are you alive?" Homer released the button on his hand receiver.

"Unless this is my ghost talking, I would say, yes, I am alive," Dusty responded. "Frank and I are at the police station in Frog's Peninsula."

Joe grabbed the receiver from Homer. "Frank? Are you all right?"

"Yes, little brother, I'm fine." Frank's voice came over the radio strong and clear. He quickly covered the events of the afternoon.

Joe breathed a sigh of relief as Frank told the story of crash-landing the sabotaged hydroplane.

"One more thing, Joe," Frank said. "I'm almost positive that giant alligator and her eggs were planted by Zack Platt to scare people away from the area."

"We'll check it out," Joe assured Frank. "Chet and I have a lot to tell you about Reuben, too. Is Deputy Miles there?"

"No, the sergeant here said she was on her way to the rodeo grounds. We're supposed to be there in less than an hour, too," Frank reminded Joe.

Joe checked his watch. It was five minutes after four, and they had planned to meet with Deputy Miles at the rodeo at five o'clock.

"We're on our way, Frank," Joe replied. "Over and out."

Frank and Dusty thanked the desk sergeant for letting them use the phone, then climbed back into their borrowed pickup truck.

As they drove down the single main street through Frog's Peninsula, Frank checked out the little seaside town. It was set on a long narrow stretch of land less than half a mile wide, bordered on one side by the Gulf of Mexico and on the other side by Florida Bay.

As they passed the marina, someone waved to them from beneath a shaded patio deck of a restaurant called the Dockside Grill. Frank squinted, trying to recognize the person. It was Salty Hubbard, the rodeo sponsor. Frank waved back.

"Do you know Salty Hubbard?" Dusty asked, seeming concerned.

"I just met him at the rodeo—" Frank started to reply.

"He's an unsavory sort," Dusty broke in. "He owns a charter boat. Local fishermen say he swindles tourists right and left. First he charges one price, then he gets the tourists out in the gulf and starts to add all these outrageous fees for bait, tackle, you name it."

As Frank caught the reflection of the Dockside Grill in the sideview mirror of the truck, he saw that Salty Hubbard had moved to the edge of the patio and was watching them drive away.

At the edge of town, they drove past a gas station called Steven's Hop and Shop. From there, it was nothing but marshland and a few scattered houses the rest of the way to the rodeo grounds.

Back at the fishing camp, Joe and Chet hurried out of the lodge. "Wait," Joe said. "I want to check out the alligator mound where I was attacked.

There might be some proof that the eggs were planted.''

"I don't think we have time for that," Chet said anxiously.

"Frank can meet with Deputy Miles, and we'll catch up with them later," Joe said as he headed toward the mass of saw grass on the western end of the little island.

Joe recognized the spot where Frank had dragged him to safety. "And then Mr. Furman walked over here and pulled back the saw grass."

Joe repeated Furman's actions, pulling back the saw grass. There was the alligator mound, all right, but something was different.

"What's going on?" Joe muttered. "The mound is starting to move!"

9 Joe Versus the Alligator

"Let's get out of here, Joe!" Chet pleaded.

Joe backed away from the pulsing mound of earth and turned to run. Suddenly he stopped, grabbing his fleeing friend by the shoulder. "Wait, Chet," Joe said, breathing a sigh of relief. "It's an alligator mound. Some of the eggs are probably hatching, that's all."

Joe knelt down to look more closely at the mound. He pushed aside the dead leaves and saw grass. The eggs were in a wide shallow hole with smooth walls. Joe noticed small orange flecks in the mud.

Inspecting one of the orange flecks, Joe realized what it was. "Rust! If an alligator dug this hole, Chet, my guess is that it used a shovel."

"Then the eggs *were* planted," Chet said. Just then, a tiny head pushed through its shell and took its first look at the world.

"Hey, little guy." Joe touched the baby alligator with his finger.

"They're cute when they're little," Chet said.

"No wonder some people want to take them home as pets." Joe smiled. Suddenly the baby alligator made a strange grunting noise.

"Why is it doing that? Is it trying to scare us off?" Chet asked.

Joe started to laugh, then got a hunch that stopped his laugh cold. "My instinct tells me we should get out of here and quick."

There was the sound of something swishing through the water to their left. As Joe and Chet turned to run, a giant alligator with one white eye emerged from the saw grass and headed for its nest—and the two boys.

"Run for it!" Joe shouted. The boys sprinted the whole way back to the fishing camp.

"We're not eaten! I mean, we're okay," Chet said, catching his breath.

"We're okay," Joe said, "but Mr. Furman has some explaining to do about how that alligator nest got where it is."

Joe looked around. Furman was the only guest missing. When they returned to the cabins, Furman was nowhere to be found.

By airboat, the ride to the Swampland Trading Post took only fifteen minutes.

Joe offered to ride Old Caloosa for the next part of their trip, but Chet had grown fond of the mule. So Joe quickly mounted Paint Can and led Frank's horse, Stonewall, behind him down the narrow highway leading to the rodeo grounds.

Joe thought that the crowd at the rodeo looked even bigger than it had the day before. He and Chet found Frank by the fire pit where the barbecue had been held.

"Where's Deputy Miles?" Joe asked.

"That's what I'd like to know," Frank replied. "She hasn't shown up, and it's already five-thirty."

While they waited, Joe told Frank all about the equipment in the poacher's cabin, the flashlight that had sunk the pedal boat, and the apparent culprit behind it all—Reuben Tallwalker.

Frank rubbed his chin. "I was certain that Zack Platt's partner was Randy Stevens. You saw them together at the trading post."

"I saw someone in a white hat with an orange-and-black feather," Joe pointed out. "Could there be two identical hats?"

Frank shook his head. "Doubtful."

"Maybe all three men are involved," Chet offered.

"And what about Trent Furman?" Joe added, filling Frank in on the conversation Joe overheard between Furman and a mystery man on the short-wave radio.

"Speaking about suspicious behavior," Joe asked, "have either of you seen Randy or Reuben?"

"The wild-bull-riding competition is going to start soon," Frank replied. "Unless they're no-shows, we should find them gearing up in the bunkhouse."

"Okay, let's head over," Joe suggested.

"You two go ahead. We can't wait for Deputy Miles any longer," Frank said. "I'm going to call in the cavalry."

"The cavalry?" Chet asked.

"Dad," the Hardys said together.

Over the years, Frank had come to the conclusion that his father, a private investigator, knew just about everyone in the detective game. If anyone could find out quickly about a bank vault that was robbed in Miami, Fenton Hardy could.

While Frank placed the call to Bayport, Joe and Chet headed to the bunkhouse where the riders dressed and prepared for their events. The place was bustling with activity when they entered. Cowboys were pulling on their boots, tying on their chaps, or rubbing ointment on their sore spots from the opening day's events. Others were playing cards at a table at the back.

Randy Stevens stepped up to one of the lockers.

When he saw Joe, he started to walk away, but Joe grabbed him by the shoulder and stopped him.

"Hey, Joe!" Randy said. "I lost track of you guys at the barbecue. What happened?"

Joe wanted to say, Cut the baloney, I saw you run away, but he was afraid to tip his hand too early. "Yeah, I don't know what happened either. By the way, Frank saw you today at the Big Cypress Alligator Farm."

"No, he didn't," Randy replied.

"That wasn't your white truck?" Joe pressed.

"I can't—" Randy stopped himself. "I mean, I don't own a truck. I've been working at the gas station all—" Randy stopped himself again, flustered.

"What gas station?" Joe asked.

"Forget it," Randy said quickly. "Listen, I've got to get to the ring. I'm riding a bull named Storm Cloud, and I need to get prepared mentally."

"Bull riding is the most dangerous competition in the rodeo," Chet pointed out. "Aren't you kind of young for that?"

"I'm eighteen!" Randy said angrily. "You just watch me."

Randy spun the dial on his combination lock and opened his locker. He began quickly searching for something, growing distressed. "Hey, where's my—"

"What?" Joe asked.

"My good-luck charm," Randy said, giving Joe and Chet an accusing look. "Someone's stolen it."

"Hey, we just got here," Chet said defensively.

"Somebody must have picked the lock."

"Who would do that?" Joe grilled Randy.

Randy didn't respond. Instead, he grabbed his hat out of his locker and turned to leave.

"Your hat!" Joe exclaimed.

"What about it?" Randy asked, puzzled.

Joe was too surprised to speak for a moment. Randy was holding a black Stetson hat with a red feather. "Where's your white hat with the orange-and-black feather?"

"Huh?" Randy was clearly confused. "Look, I've got to go." Randy pushed by Joe and out the side door leading to the bull pens.

"Why would Randy change hats?" Joe wondered aloud. "Does he know that we're on to him?"

"He must know," Chet remarked. "A few simple questions about his driving a white truck and being too young for bull riding and he practically jumped out of his skin."

"Joe!" Frank shouted, rushing in. "Dad just gave me some incredible news. I think I know what they're looking for in Gator Swamp. It turns out the robbers didn't steal currency from that bank vault in Miami."

"What did they steal?" Chet asked.

Lights went off in Joe's head. Frank opened his

mouth to respond, but Joe beat him to it. "Gold coins."

Frank stared at his brother, baffled. "Yes! Half a million dollars in rare gold coins. How did you know?"

"Reuben's metal detector, Deputy Miles saying she didn't have to worry about the loot floating off, and then the gold coin Randy was flipping last night," Joe explained. "It suddenly all fits together."

"Yeah," Frank said. "We need to get a closer look at Randy's coin, and pronto."

Chet and Joe glanced at each other, frowning.

"Randy says somebody stole his coin out of his locker," Joe explained.

"He said they picked his lock," Chet added, pointing to Randy's locker.

Frank examined the lock. "This is a heavy-duty lock. To pick a lock like this, you'd have to know your stuff."

"You mean you'd have to be a locksmith?" Chet asked.

"A locksmith," Frank said with a grin, "or a safecracker!"

10 Live Robbers and Lost Gold

"You're right! One of the robbers who drowned must have been a safecracker," Chet said.

"What if the robbers didn't drown?" Frank asked his companions.

"If their stolen airboat was found at the bottom of Florida Bay," Joe pointed out, "it's safe to assume they drowned."

"And if they survived, what would they be doing back in Gator Swamp?" Chet asked.

Frank was ready with a hunch. "The robbers knew they were being pursued. What if they ditched the evidence? What if they hid the coins in the swamp?"

"Then they wouldn't have to search," Joe said. "They could have gone right back to the spot and

81

recovered them, unless—" Joe stopped midsentence as an idea struck him. "With the wind and rough water of the winter storm, the coins could have been knocked overboard!"

"Little brother, sometimes your hunches surprise even me," Frank said, slapping Joe on the shoulder.

"Wait a second," Chet argued. "What makes you think Randy's telling the truth about his coin being stolen? We're pretty sure he's lied to us about everything else."

"Chet's right, Frank," Joe admitted.

"Hmm." Frank thought it over. "If anyone would know who Randy Stevens is, I'm looking at him," he said, eyeing a card player at the back of the bunkhouse. Joe turned to look. It took him a moment to recognize Barney Quick, the rodeo clown, without his white makeup and red ten-gallon hat.

"Mr. Quick?" Frank said, approaching the table. "We're sorry to interrupt your game, but we were interested in one of the rodeo contestants. What can you tell us about Randy Stevens?"

"Nothing," Quick replied.

"Nothing?" Chet repeated.

"Well, I know an Ernie Stevens," Quick recalled, playing a card. "He moved to Frog's Peninsula a year ago. Runs the all-night service station. He has a boy at the junior high, I think. But the boy wouldn't be old enough to ride rodeo."

"Randy must have ridden rodeo somewhere," Joe insisted.

"I'd say no," Quick replied. "But if you don't believe me, check the book."

"The book?" Chet asked.

"The rodeo book. Mr. Deeter's got it," Quick explained. "It'll have names and statistics on any rodeo in America." Quick tossed his cards on the table. "If you'll excuse me, boys, I have to get into my makeup."

The boys thanked Barney Quick as he headed out through the side door.

"I'll ask Mr. Deeter about that book," Frank suggested. "You and Chet better get into the grandstands. We don't want to miss Dusty's ride."

"But we still haven't found Reuben," Joe said.

"Maybe he's afraid to show up," Chet reasoned.

"Reuben, afraid?" Joe shook his head. "No way. He's got to be around here someplace. Go ahead, Chet, and save us some good seats."

The three boys split up. Frank caught Melvin Deeter just as he was leaving his trailer and asked about looking at the rodeo book.

"I have to get to the announcer's booth at the main ring," Deeter replied. He saw the concerned look on Frank's face. "Is it something connected to that bank robbery?"

"I'm afraid it is," Frank replied.

Deeter paused. Then he unlocked his door, stepped in, grabbed a thick book off his desk, and

83

handed it to Frank. "Be careful with it, son. Bring it to me in the announcer's booth when you're finished."

Frank found some good light near the concession stand, and he began rapidly skimming through the lists of rodeos all over America. Ten minutes later he slammed the book shut and went off to find Chet and Joe.

Frank found Chet by the bulletin board where the entries and results were posted. Chet had a half-eaten corn dog in his hand and a puzzled look on his face. "What's wrong, Chet?"

Chet turned to Frank. "I can't find his name."

"Neither can I," Frank said. "I've checked every rodeo in the last three years. Randy Stevens is nowhere—"

"Not Randy Stevens," Chet interrupted. "Trent Furman."

"What?" Frank asked.

"I was hanging around the bulletin board hoping to scare up a steer-roping partner," Chet explained, "and I started looking at the board. Mr. Furman's been bragging about winning the bronco-busting trophy at the rodeo in Fargo, North Dakota, but he didn't even enter the competition here."

Frank's eyes widened. "Wait a second!" Frank started paging through the rodeo book.

"In fact," Chet added, "he isn't entered in a single category."

"Here it is!" Frank exclaimed. "The Fargo Rodeo." He paused. "Trent Furman not only didn't win the bronco-busting competition, he never even competed."

Joe had searched all over the rodeo grounds, but no one had seen Reuben Tallwalker since the day before.

He was passing the bull pens when he thought he heard someone whispering. He stopped and listened. He heard snorts and huffs from the huge animals, then the whispering again.

Crouching down, Joe moved silently along the fence until he came to a pen with the name Señor Cyclone hanging on the gate. Inside the pen was a huge charcoal gray bull.

Whispering into the animal's ear was Reuben Tallwalker. "You are a great warrior, but you will not throw me. Tonight is mine." Reuben cocked his head, listening. "Someone is outside your gate, skulking about like a weasel."

Joe stood up tall. "I'm not skulking. I just didn't want you to run away from me again."

With one smooth motion, Reuben pulled himself up and over the gate, until he stood face-to-face with Joe. "I'm not running."

"Neither am I," Joe replied. "Here, you dropped this." Joe handed Reuben his rodeo number. "Forty-five. That's yours, right?"

Reuben slipped it in his pocket. "So?"

"We found it in the woods beside the highway

last night. You lost it while you were following us,"
Joe accused him.

"Why didn't you come get me?" Reuben
taunted. "Were you afraid?"

"Last night it was too dark," Joe replied. "This
afternoon, I didn't like the look of the machete you
were carrying."

"This afternoon?" Reuben asked. "So you were
out in the swamp again today. That was your
equipment in the poacher's shack," Reuben accused.

"*Our* equipment?" Joe said in disbelief. "Why
would we have a snorkeling mask and a metal
detector?"

Reuben's eyes narrowed. "So you could search
for arrowheads or some lost Seminole treasure you
think is there. Desecrating an island that was
sacred to my forefathers."

"You've got the wrong guys and the wrong crime,
Reuben," Joe explained.

Reuben wasn't listening. "Dusty Cole respects
our island, but not you and your snooping brother."

Joe protested. "My brother and I are trying to
find the people responsible for a bank heist!"

"You're a liar," Reuben broke in.

"Ask your grandfather," Joe replied. "He knows
that we meant no harm."

"I called you a liar," Reuben repeated.

Joe could tell Reuben was looking for a fight, and

he was ready to give it to him. "I'm giving you three seconds to take that back," Joe added hotly.

"Hey, what's going on here!" One of Deeter's cowhands moved in quickly between Joe and Reuben. "The bull riding is about to start. Isn't that enough excitement for you boys?"

"We'll continue this later," Reuben said as he stormed off to the rodeo ring.

"I'm looking forward to it," Joe replied coolly.

As much as he wanted to clock Reuben one to the jaw, Joe found it hard to believe that the proud young man could be a bank robber or a safecracker.

"It's about time!" Chet said as Joe sat down with him and Frank in the grandstands. "Four riders have already gone, and not one stayed on his bull's back long enough to qualify."

"I found Reuben," Joe replied. "He actually accused us of owning the equipment in the poacher's shack."

"Doesn't surprise me," Chet grumbled. "No one tells the truth about anything around here."

Chet and Frank explained what they had discovered about Randy Stevens and Trent Furman not having been listed in a single rodeo.

"So Furman is a fraud, and maybe Randy, too," Joe said.

"Don't forget Reuben," Chet added.

"The thing is, Chet," Joe said, "I almost believe Reuben."

"Why?" Chet asked. "Who else would have snorkeling equipment and a metal detector in Reuben's shack?"

The answer suddenly hit Joe. "Zack Platt! Of course! He asked about snorkeling equipment the day we got here. He could have easily stolen Tallwalker's flashlight while my back was turned. He used the poacher's shack to store his equipment because someone—like Randy—told him it was abandoned."

Frank picked up the story. "And instead of hunting Big Bertha in Gator Swamp last night, he was searching for the coins with the metal detector."

"Right," Joe concurred.

"It's a solid theory, Joe," Frank said. "Now we need to prove it."

"The next contestant is . . ." Deeter's voice echoed through the public-address system. "Dusty Cole riding Texas Twister!"

"Come on, Dusty!" Chet shouted.

The boys could see Dusty lowering himself onto the bull's back. He wound the guide rope tightly around his gloved hand, then nodded to one of the rodeo clowns that he was ready. The rodeo clown swung the gate wide open.

Texas Twister was as good as his name. The bull jerked and twisted like a whirling tornado, kicking up dirt in every direction. Dusty couldn't have been happier. Giving his trademark whoop and holler, he hung on through the qualifying bell and got a massive round of applause from the crowd.

"Way to go, Dusty!" Frank shouted. Dusty tipped his hat to the three boys and smiled.

"Good ride, Dusty!" Deeter added over the public-address system. "Our next contestant is Randy Stevens, riding Storm Cloud."

Three pairs of eyes snapped over to the pen where Randy was lowering himself onto the bull's back. He held up his hand, letting the rodeo clown know he wasn't ready.

"He looks awfully scared," Chet pointed out.

"Yeah," Frank agreed. "But is he scared about the bull or about something else?"

Randy took a deep breath, then grabbed the guide rope and was about to loop it around his gloved hand when Barney Quick suddenly swung the gate wide open.

Storm Cloud blasted out into the ring, bucking wildly and yanking the guide rope out of Randy's hand. There were screams and shouts from the crowd. Randy was helpless, having nothing to hold on to except for the bull's hide.

Suddenly Storm Cloud spun completely around in midair, hurling Randy off his back and into the fence. The crowd gasped in horror.

"Mr. Quick isn't doing anything to help Randy!" Chet shouted, pointing toward the gate.

Frank spotted the rodeo clown running out of the ring and toward the bunkhouse, shielding his face with his ten-gallon hat. "This may have been a setup!" Frank shouted.

"Or a frame-up. Come on, guys!" Joe yelled. The Hardys ran down the steps of the grandstands and vaulted over the railing into the ring. Chet followed close behind.

Joe saw Randy trying to get to his feet. Stunned, he fell back to one knee. Storm Cloud had turned and was bearing down on the dazed teenager. Joe gave a loud whistle and waved his hands frantically, trying to get the bull's attention.

Storm Cloud turned toward the noise. Frank and Chet rushed to Randy, helping him over to the fence, where two cowhands pulled him to safety.

"Uh-oh," Joe muttered as Storm Cloud lowered his head and charged. Joe ran full steam toward the closest railing. He heard the bull snorting behind him and felt its hot breath on his back.

Joe knew he was about to be sandwiched between the fence and the bull's deadly horns.

At the last second, Joe jumped. He grasped the top railing and pulled up his feet just as the bull's horns crashed against the slats of the fence below him.

Storm Cloud hit the fence with such force that it shook Joe's grip loose, and he fell down into the ring and onto his back.

Joe saw Frank behind the bull, shouting, trying to

get the bull's attention, but Storm Cloud was now focused on the younger Hardy. Joe made a break for the other side of the ring.

But the distance was too far, and the bull was too fast. Storm Cloud was catching Joe, and he knew he would never make it to the fence in time.

11 A Lot of Bull

"Faster, Joe!" Frank shouted across the ring. But Joe was running as fast as he could through the deep, soft dirt in the ring.

Suddenly Storm Cloud stumbled as Chet's lasso wrapped around the bull's hind leg. It was the break Joe needed. "Way to go, Chet!" he shouted, as he took a flying leap toward the top railing and managed to pull himself up to safety.

Meanwhile, Chet was being jerked around the ring in every direction. Yanked off his feet and dragged through the dirt, he lost his grip on the rope.

"Over here, Chet!" Joe shouted, motioning for his friend to run toward him.

Chet jumped, grabbing a slat halfway up the

fence. Joe leaned over, pulling on Chet's wrist with all his might, and yanked him over the fence just as Storm Cloud crashed into the spot where Chet had been.

Seeing his friend and his brother out of danger, Frank climbed the fence to safety. Finally two other rodeo clowns ran into the ring through a second gate and got the bull under control.

By the time Frank reached the other side of the grandstand to join Joe and Chet, Dusty had heard about the accident and rushed over from the bunkhouse.

Everyone was standing around Randy Stevens, who was being attended to by a paramedic.

"What happened?" Dusty asked.

"One of the rodeo clowns accidentally swung open the gate too soon," a spectator explained.

"It was no accident," Frank said to Dusty. "The clown took off running right after he did it."

"Which clown?" Dusty asked.

"Barney Quick," an older spectator said. "I recognized his ten-gallon hat."

"The ten-gallon hat that he used to hide his face," Frank whispered to Joe.

"You're right," Joe replied. "We never got a good look at him."

The paramedic tending to Randy rose to his feet. "He's breathing, but he's lost consciousness," the paramedic explained. "We'd better get him to the hospital on Frog's Peninsula."

A second paramedic brought a stretcher from the ambulance that was stationed behind the rodeo ring for just such emergencies. The two paramedics carefully moved Randy onto the stretcher.

"Come on, everyone. Let's find Barney Quick," Dusty instructed.

"I'm going with Randy to the hospital," Frank said to Joe and Chet as the crowd dispersed.

"Good thinking," Joe said. "We have to grill him about the gold coin and find out why someone tried to knock him off."

"That's only part of the reason I'm going," Frank replied. "I also want to make sure he's okay."

"You're showing a lot of sympathy for someone we suspect robbed a bank vault and sabotaged the hydroplane," Joe remarked.

"You jumped into the ring to save him as quickly as I did," Frank pointed out.

Joe paused, then nodded. "Randy doesn't seem capable of that kind of crime, does he? He talks tough, but deep down he seems afraid."

"There's no doubt Randy's hiding something," Frank said. "I hope I'll find out what it is tonight."

"Go ahead, Frank," Chet jumped in. "Joe and I can help Dusty find Barney Quick."

Frank hurried toward the parking lot and caught the paramedic as he was getting into the ambulance with Randy.

Frank knew he had to lie, or he would never be

allowed to ride in the ambulance. "I'm Frank, um, Stevens, Randy's brother."

"Oh," the paramedic replied, "I didn't know he had a family member here. Come on along, then." Frank climbed into the back of the ambulance with Randy.

As the driver turned on the siren and sped away, Frank looked at Randy's face. Lying there quietly, his eyes and mouth closed, he looked more like a young kid than a ruthless criminal.

Chet and Joe headed after Dusty, who had led most of the search party toward the bunkhouse— the direction in which the rodeo clown had been seen running.

Joe suddenly stopped short and snapped his fingers. "Wait! When we talked with Mr. Quick in the bunkhouse, he said he had to go put on his makeup. That means he would have gone to his trailer."

"The clown's trailer is at the end of the parking lot," Chet said. "But why look there?"

"Frank had a hunch that it might not have been Barney Quick in the ring," Joe replied, "and I have a hunch how we can find out."

When they opened the door to the trailer used by Barney Quick and his team, they discovered the place in a shambles, as if there had been a struggle.

Makeup and clothing were thrown everywhere.

One of the pairs of baggy overalls on the floor suddenly moved, and the boys heard a groan.

Joe picked up the overall, revealing Barney Quick, dazed, and with his hand over a large bump on his head. "What—" he said, then saw Joe and Chet. "Why'd you hit me?"

"We didn't hit you, Mr. Quick," Chet explained. "It was someone else."

"I was at my makeup table. . . ." Quick trailed off, not fully conscious yet. "What did they steal?"

"My guess is the only thing they stole was your identity," Joe replied.

"Huh?" Quick asked.

"Your wig, your hat, and your costume," Chet clarified.

"What's in your hand?" Joe had spotted a piece of blue-and-white flannel material in Quick's left hand.

"That's right," Quick recalled. "I fought with whoever it was, ripped off their pocket before they clunked me on the head."

"Did you see who it was?" Chet asked. Quick shook his head.

"Do you recognize this material?" Joe wondered.

Quick shook his head again. "A lot of cowboys wear flannel shirts."

"His pocket!" An idea struck Joe. "If there was anything in the pocket, it could have fallen out when the pocket was ripped off."

Joe scanned the floor of the trailer. He spotted a folded piece of paper.

"What's on it?" Chet asked as Joe picked up the paper.

"A note," Joe replied, and read aloud the words scrawled on the paper: "'The kid can't be trusted. Take care of it.'"

"What does it mean?" Quick asked, confused.

Joe shared a solemn look with Chet. "It means that someone was trying to get Randy Stevens out of the way."

Joe quickly figured out a plan. "Chet, stay here with Mr. Quick. I'll send some help."

"Where are you going?" Chet asked.

"I have to track down the phony rodeo clown before he gets away!" Joe called over his shoulder, as he rushed out the door of the trailer.

As Joe ran toward the bunkhouse, he heard Melvin Deeter on the public-address system telling the crowd that the bull-riding competition would be postponed until officials could investigate the circumstances of Randy Stevens's accident.

Joe ran into Dusty and a few cowhands in front of the bunkhouse, and he told them about Barney Quick.

"Well, whoever the phony is, he zipped through the front door of the bunkhouse and out the back before anyone got a look at him," Dusty said to Joe. "We're headed for the main tent."

Dusty and the others hurried on. Joe decided to think before he moved, trying to imagine where he would hide on the rodeo grounds if he were a criminal.

His eyes settled on a huge dark building looming near the far edge of the rodeo grounds. "The barn!" he said aloud. Near the corner of the barn, Joe saw a figure beneath a hanging lantern, kneeling over something.

Joe sprinted toward the barn. The figure beneath the lantern rose to his feet. Joe recognized the multicolored woven jacket. It was Reuben.

Joe was still fifty yards away when Reuben walked cautiously inside the barn. Reuben didn't seem to be in a hurry, like someone trying to escape. In fact, Joe doubted Reuben could have seen him approaching because Reuben's back was turned.

Joe stopped at the corner of the barn, wanting to see what Reuben had been kneeling over. It was a red ten-gallon hat and a clown wig. Barney Quick's costume, Joe thought to himself.

Peering into the open door of the barn, Joe saw nothing but blackness. He stepped up onto a nearby barrel and grabbed the lantern hanging on a hook above him and ventured into the vast two-story structure.

Joe could hear the breathing, snorting, and whinnying of some of the broncos in their stalls. The horses' names were posted on signs beside each stable door.

Joe walked past Diablo, Pecos Bill, and Thunderbolt. Ahead, he recognized Volcano as the name of the horse Reuben had ridden in the competition. As Joe passed Volcano's stall, he heard a small jingle.

Moving toward the sound, he discovered a set of spurs hanging on a nail beside Volcano's stall. They were moving slightly, as if someone had just passed by.

Suddenly Joe heard the crack of a bullwhip. He winced in pain as the whip lashed his right hand, forcing him to drop the lantern. The lantern broke on the ground, setting the hay-covered floor on fire.

Before he could smother the flames, rough hands grabbed Joe from behind and pushed him into Volcano's stall.

Volcano reared up, whinnying and lashing forward with its front hooves. As Joe held up his arms to shield his face, he could feel the intense heat from the fire raging just outside the stall.

With no room to maneuver inside the stall, Joe thought the safest place for him now would be on Volcano's back. Grabbing Volcano's mane, Joe tried to hoist himself up, but the horse reared and kicked again. A hoof struck Joe directly over his right eye and knocked him down.

Lying on his back, stunned, Joe was barely aware

of the blurry orange flame creeping underneath the door into the stall.

Suddenly the stall door swung open. Joe rolled to the side, dodging Volcano as the horse raced by him. Someone grabbed Joe by the wrists and began dragging him across the barn floor.

Joe coughed, trying to get oxygen. The smoke was so thick that he could hardly breathe, and he could not see the face of his rescuer. The last thing Joe saw before he passed out was the multicolored sleeve of a woven jacket.

"Joe?" came a voice.

Joe opened his eyes, regaining consciousness. "Chet!" he said to his old friend kneeling over him.

"Are you okay?" Chet asked.

"Yeah, I just breathed too much smoke," Joe replied, looking around to get his bearings. He was lying outside the barn, propped up against a saddle.

Dozens of rodeo riders and spectators were running in every direction, releasing the horses trapped in their stalls, dragging hoses, filling buckets with water, and doing anything they could to douse the fire in the barn.

"What happened to your head?" Chet asked.

Joe felt the cut over his eye where the horse had kicked him, and he told Chet about seeing Reuben standing over the stolen clown costume and following him into the barn.

"I was thrown into Volcano's stall," Joe continued, "then someone else came in and pulled me to safety."

"Who?" Chet asked.

"I don't know who put me in there, but I think it was Reuben Tallwalker who got me out," Joe replied.

"Reuben?" Chet echoed. Then he added, "Wow."

Joe got to his feet and looked around. "But where is Reuben now?" Neither he nor Chet could spot him among the people fighting the fire.

"Over there," Chet said, pointing behind the barn. At the edge of the fire, Joe saw Reuben running across the meadow toward the wooded swampland.

"We're following him this time," Joe vowed. Borrowing flashlights from two cowhands, the pair headed off toward the swamp.

The pitch-darkness was broken only by the narrow beam of Joe's flashlight. After a moment's pause at the edge of the woods, the two teenagers plunged into the eerie darkness of the vine-tangled swampland.

12 The Real Randy Stevens

Joe heard sucking noises up ahead. He thought they sounded like someone walking through thick muck. He picked up the pace, shining the flashlight beam ahead of him, catching glimpses of Reuben zigzagging through the thick underbrush forty yards ahead of him.

Joe had been pursuing Reuben for ten minutes before it struck him that he hadn't heard Chet's voice in a while. "Chet?" he called quietly, turning back to look and listen. No answer.

Joe wondered whether he should stay on Reuben's trail or backtrack to find his friend. Before he could decide, he heard the voices of two men approaching from the opposite direction. Joe turned off his flashlight and ducked behind a tree.

"He's following us," came a deep voice, shining the beam of his flashlight across the dense underbrush. Joe recognized it as Zack Platt's voice.

"Double back that way," the second man ordered. It was a high-pitched voice that sounded familiar, but Joe couldn't immediately identify it.

Joe pressed himself against the tree and held his breath. As the men were passing, Joe caught sight of Reuben Tallwalker, crouched beside a fallen tree not more than five feet from Joe.

Reuben put his finger to his lips, signaling Joe to stay quiet. Twenty feet to their left, Zack Platt hacked through the underbrush with a machete, looking for Reuben, Joe, or, Joe thought, both of them.

After Platt was a safe distance away, Joe crawled over to Reuben, not sure whether to hit him or shake his hand.

"You want to explain all this?" Joe whispered.

"After the accident at the ring, I saw the rodeo clown throw off his disguise at the barn, then race inside," Reuben began. "So I followed him."

"Who threw me into Volcano's stall?" Joe pressed.

"Two men," Reuben explained.

"Did you see their faces?" Joe asked.

"No. It was dark and I was too far away," Reuben replied. "But one of them had a red beard."

"Zack Platt," Joe said. "He's posing as an alligator trapper, but we think he may be a bank robber as well."

Reuben nodded. "The other man wore a white hat."

"With an orange-and-black feather?" Joe asked.

Reuben nodded again.

"It couldn't have been Randy Stevens. He's in the hospital," Joe said.

Joe saw Reuben looking at him quizzically. "I'll explain it to you later," Joe said.

"Zack Platt is the man who has been snooping around Twin Cypress Key?" Reuben asked with anger in his voice.

"Probably. But I wouldn't mess with him, Reuben," Joe warned. "Zack Platt is as strong as an ox."

Suddenly two hundred pounds of muscle fell on Joe's back. "Oh, I'm *stronger* than an ox!" Platt laughed.

Reuben got up to help Joe, but he was tackled to the ground by a man in a white hat.

Platt pulled Joe up by the hair and held a machete to his throat. "What do you think you're doing out here, boy?"

Joe answered with a hard elbow to Platt's stomach, doubling the larger man over, allowing himself a chance to escape.

Joe didn't want to leave Reuben, but he knew the smartest move now was to get back to the rodeo grounds and find help.

Moving as fast as he could through the swampland, Joe spotted a tree stump in his path. He hurdled over the stump, but his foot did not hit solid ground on the other side. Instead, he sank up to his thigh in muddy water. As Joe sank another foot down, he realized he had not landed in mud or in water. It was quicksand!

He knew he only had seconds to think of a way out of this jam. He tried to pump his legs, hoping to slow his descent into the quicksand. About three feet overhead, he spotted the low branch of a mangrove tree.

Undoing his belt, Joe tried to hook it over the top of the branch. His first attempt failed. On his second attempt, he got closer, but the buckle bounced off the limb.

Joe sank another few inches. With all his strength, he stretched out and swung the belt one last time. It hooked over the mangrove branch above him.

Stretching up with his other hand, he grabbed the buckle and slowly began pulling himself out of the quicksand.

A flashlight beam suddenly blinded him. "Help me!" the younger Hardy shouted in desperation.

The figure holding the flashlight stepped up to the edge of the quicksand pit. The direct beam in his eyes made it impossible for Joe to make out who it was, but he did catch a glimpse of moonlight reflecting off a white hat.

Without a word, the figure grabbed the mangrove branch with one hand. Joe reached out to grab the man's free hand.

Instead, the man pulled the branch with his full weight until it snapped, then dropped the branch into the quicksand pit.

"Wait!" Joe pleaded.

But the man in the white hat simply dusted the dirt off his hands and walked away.

Joe tried to use the broken branch to drag himself out of the pit, but it wasn't long enough to reach the solid ground. Joe sank down to his shoulders. He pushed the branch deep into the quicksand, hoping to prop himself up, but the branch never touched bottom.

The quicksand was up to his chin now. As he sank deeper, Joe Hardy was out of options and he knew it.

"His name is Randy Stevens, and he lives right here on Frog's Peninsula," Frank informed the admissions nurse at the hospital.

"And you're his brother?" the nurse asked.

Frank felt uncomfortable about lying again. "Well, I'm . . . *like* his brother. I'm a good friend."

"The doctor says he has some deep bruises and possibly a mild concussion," the nurse explained. "You shouldn't worry. By the way, how old is your friend?"

"Eighteen," Frank replied.

The nurse punched in Randy's name on her

computer to see if the hospital had him on file. "Yes, here he is. Randy Stevens. Seven Manatee Lane. He had his tonsils out last year."

"Last year?" Frank asked, puzzled, remembering that he and most of his friends had had that operation as children. "He had his tonsils removed when he was seventeen?"

"No," the nurse replied, "when he was thirteen."

Frank and the nurse shared a quizzical look. "Does it show his birth date on your records?" Frank asked.

"Uh-huh," the nurse responded. "According to his file, Randy Stevens will be turning fifteen one week from today."

Frank's brain scrambled, trying to figure out this latest twist in the deepening mystery of Gator Swamp. "Thank you," he said to the nurse. "Where's the nearest pay phone?"

Frank dialed the Frog's Peninsula Police Department. Deputy Miles wasn't there, nor had she been heard from since that afternoon.

"Does anyone have a clue about where she might have gone?" Frank asked the desk sergeant.

"She went off-duty at one o'clock this afternoon," the sergeant explained. "She said she was headed to the rodeo."

"And that's all she said?" Frank pressed.

"Yes, that's all she said," the sergeant replied. Then he added, "Oh, wait. She said she was stopping by the marina to double-check on something first."

"The marina? Well, thank you, Sergeant," Frank said, and hung up. For now, he would have to investigate on his own. He hurried to the room where they had left Randy to recuperate.

The light in Randy's room was off. Frank knew he should probably let the teenager rest, but he had to get some answers.

"Randy?" Frank called quietly. There was no answer. "Randy?" No answer again. Frank flipped on the light switch next to the door. The hospital bed was empty. Randy Stevens was gone.

13 In the Nick of Time

"Help!" Joe shouted in a last-ditch effort to save himself.

A lasso suddenly landed neatly atop the surface of the quicksand. "Grab it, Joe!" a familiar voice called.

Joe grabbed the rope, and Chet began to tug. "It feels like you weigh three hundred pounds." Chet groaned.

Slowly Chet dragged Joe's quicksand-caked body onto solid ground, then fell backward. Chet and Joe sat for a minute, huffing and puffing, trying to catch their breath.

"Chet? Did I ever tell you how glad I am that you took up your new hobby?" Joe said between breaths.

"No," Chet replied, laughing. "Did I ever tell you that I think you've set the record for the most changes of clothes in two days?"

Joe laughed, then grew serious. "Come on, Chet. We need to get back to the rodeo. I think Zack Platt and his accomplice have Reuben."

"I thought Reuben *was* Mr. Platt's accomplice," Chet said.

"No," Joe replied. "I have a lot to tell you."

As the two boys headed back through the swamp toward the rodeo grounds, Joe told Chet about his encounter with Reuben and of the mysteries that were starting to become clearer to him now.

"So Reuben's been following us because he really did think we were the ones messing around on his ancestors' sacred island," Chet said.

"Right," Joe replied.

"But if Zack Platt's accomplice isn't Reuben and isn't Randy Stevens, who is the man in the white hat?" Chet wondered aloud.

"I think I have an idea," Joe replied.

By the time the two boys made it back to the barn, the fire had been put out. Tired cowboys sat on the ground outside the half-burned structure. One cowboy, his face covered with soot, jumped to his feet when he saw Joe and Chet walking up.

"Where in Sam Hill have you been!" Dusty shouted, giving his young friends a hug. "I thought you had burned up."

Deeter, Homer, and some of the other cowboys

surrounded Joe and Chet, relieved to see them alive. Joe explained about his near-fatal encounter in the swampland.

"Thanks to Chet, I escaped," Joe concluded. "But I think they got Reuben."

"They?" Deeter asked. "Who exactly is 'they'?"

"Zack Platt and his accomplice," Joe replied. "Find Zack Platt and you'll have your culprit."

"Why don't you say that to my face, youngster?" Joe whirled around to find himself face-to-face with Zack Platt. Standing beside Platt was Trent Furman.

"All right," Joe replied, his temper flaring. "Explain why Reuben Tallwalker saw you and another man run from the barn after you'd thrown me into Volcano's stall?"

"What are you talking about, kid?" Platt countered. "I'm the one who saw young Tallwalker running from the barn after he had started the fire."

"He didn't start the fire, you did!" Joe shot back.

"Hold on, Joe," Furman jumped in. "You're the one I saw walk into that barn with a lantern."

"Don't listen to him. He's a fraud," Chet shouted, pointing an accusing finger at Furman. "He didn't win a rodeo in Fargo, he's never even *been* in a rodeo, and we can prove it!"

The crowd quieted, looking to Furman for an explanation.

"You don't need to prove it," Furman said, acting embarrassed. "I told a few tall tales. What cowboy doesn't? I didn't want everyone to know I was a greenhorn, that's all."

Joe couldn't believe that the crowd was buying Furman's story. "He's lying! Furman and Platt are the robbers who cracked the bank vault in Miami."

Furman laughed. "Do you mean the robbers that the Coast Guard is dragging the bottom of the bay for?"

A few cowboys chuckled at this. Joe grew even angrier. "Trent Furman is the man who left me to sink in quicksand about ten minutes ago!"

Deeter gave Joe a stern look. "Ten minutes ago, Mr. Furman was standing toe-to-toe with me helping put out the fire in the barn. He's been with me from the time the blaze started."

Suddenly all eyes were looking accusingly at the two boys. Joe knew he had blown it. No one would doubt Mr. Deeter's word, and Joe and Chet had lost all credibility.

"I think you owe Mr. Furman and Mr. Platt an apology," Deeter said.

"I'm sorry," Joe said, mustering as much sincerity as he could.

"I'll call the authorities and have them investigate the matter," Mr. Deeter assured the crowd.

"Good idea," Platt said, flashing a mean smile at Joe. "If you'll excuse me now, I still have an alligator to catch tonight."

"What about the rodeo?" Billy Biggs asked Deeter.

"Postponed until further notice," Deeter said.

The crowd grumbled, disappointed.

"Look, I'm sorry," Deeter said, "but there's another storm headed our way late tonight. We'll have to see what it does before I can tell you if we'll be back in business tomorrow."

"If a storm's coming, we'd better get back to the fishing camp and batten down the hatches," Homer suggested.

Everyone kicked into high gear. While the cowhands began closing down the rodeo, Homer and the other spectators headed for the parking lot.

Dusty stopped to talk with Joe and Chet. "Boys, I believe there's all kinds of criminal mischief going on."

"I'm glad someone believes us," Joe said thankfully.

"I wasn't finished," Dusty said. "You're going to get us all in trouble making claims without hard evidence and the law on your side."

"You're right," Joe admitted.

"You can trust Mr. Deeter," Dusty went on. "He'll have this whole thing investigated thoroughly."

Homer pulled up in the pickup truck, which was filled with the other fishing-camp guests. "Come on, Dusty, I want to get back before the storm hits."

Joe looked over the guests in the bed of the truck and realized who was missing. "Where's Mr. Furman?"

Homer gave Joe a cross look. "He said he'd had enough of our hospitality and is taking a motel room in Frog's Peninsula for the night."

With that, Homer pulled away, kicking up dust as he headed down the road.

As Joe and Chet walked toward the bunkhouse, Joe went over in his mind that first night at the rodeo. If Trent Furman wasn't the man in the white hat, whom had Randy borrowed it from? Joe stopped dead as they passed the fire pit behind the main tent.

"What's wrong?" Chet asked.

"There's a third man," Joe said, half to himself.

"What?" Chet was still confused.

"Are you up for a long ride on Old Caloosa?" Joe asked. "I think I've finally figured out who the man in the white hat is."

Frank figured he had walked about a mile from the hospital when he reached 7 Manatee Lane. The little house was dark inside. Apparently, Randy was not there.

As Frank walked around back, he noted that the house was on the waterfront. Frank moved to the seawall and looked out at the dark waters of Florida Bay. He saw a few distant lights, which he guessed came from Dusty's fishing camp.

Randy's dock had a hoist for a small boat. Frank figured his best move was to watch for Randy from the dock. This way he'd also have a good view of Randy's house.

Frank checked his watch. It was three minutes past ten. He sat down, listening to the tiny waves breaking against the seawall. A cool breeze whipped up, and he wondered if it meant rain was coming.

Frank was dead tired, and the breeze and the sound of the waves made him doze off for a minute. At least, he thought it was for a minute until he checked his watch again. It was eleven-thirty!

He heard the low hum of a small outboard motor on the water. The sound grew louder as it moved toward him. Frank took cover behind a palm tree.

The outboard engine shut off, and Frank saw a johnboat heading toward the dock. In it was Randy.

Frank arched his eyebrow, puzzled. Why would Randy go all the way back to the Swampland Trading Post for his boat when the hospital was only a mile from his house, he wondered. Even if Randy were too young to drive, he could easily walk that distance.

Randy hoisted the boat out of the water, then headed toward the house.

Frank knew he had to be cautious. Even if Randy was only fourteen, he was nearly as tall as Frank and looked just as strong. Frank slipped up behind Randy and stuck a knuckle in his back. "Freeze!"

Randy went rigid. "Don't hurt me, please. I didn't tell anyone about the gold coin, I swear."

Frank quickly frisked Randy to make sure he wasn't armed. Randy sneaked a look at Frank out of the corner of his eye and saw that the "gun" was only Frank's knuckle.

"You!" Randy spun around and pushed Frank away. "With your snooping around, you nearly got me killed!"

Randy threw a wild punch, but Frank easily ducked under it. He let Randy swing again, and using his opponent's momentum, he threw the boy onto the grass. Randy grabbed a coconut from beneath the palm. As funny as Randy looked coming at Frank with a green coconut, Frank knew that the coconut was as hard as a rock and could do as much damage.

Frank made an X with his arms, blocking Randy's blow, then flipped the lanky teenager onto the ground, pulling Randy's right arm behind his back and putting it in an unbreakable hold.

"I'm not letting you up until I get some answers. And this time, Randy, the answers are going to be the truth. How old are you?"

"Eighteen!" Randy shouted, squirming to get away.

"How old?" Frank asked, adding a little pressure to the arm hold.

"Fourteen!" Randy shouted, grimacing. "Look, all I did was find a gold coin in Gator Swamp," he said. "I didn't know it was part of a Seminole treasure."

"A Seminole treasure?" Frank asked.

"He said he would split it with me if I kept quiet," Randy explained.

"Who did?" Frank pressed.

"I can't say," Randy insisted. "He'll kill me."

"First off, Randy, whoever it is, someone tried to kill you anyway," Frank told him. "And secondly, your coin isn't part of a Seminole treasure. The Seminoles never minted gold coins."

Hearing this, Randy stopped squirming. "What do you mean?"

"I mean, he was lying to you," Frank replied. "My guess is that gold coin you found came from a bank vault in Miami, and there's half a million dollars' worth of them still lost in Gator Swamp."

"Wow," Randy said heavily. "I had no idea. You can let go of me, Frank. I won't fight you anymore."

Frank let Randy up. Dusting off his clothes, Randy began to explain his bizarre behavior. "My father owns the all-night gas station on the main road out of town. He won't let me ride rodeo, even though he knows I look old enough to pass for eighteen at least."

"Which is the minimum age for contestants in the Swampland Rodeo," Frank surmised.

"Right. I'm sure Dad won't let me ride even when I am eighteen," Randy said. "He's always afraid I'm going to get hurt."

Frank gave Randy a skeptical look, throwing a glance at the discolored bump on Randy's head.

Randy touched the bump and continued. "Anyway, I couldn't get past the gas station without Dad or one of his friends seeing me, so I would take my boat through Gator Swamp and walk from the trading post."

"You must really love the rodeo to take that kind of risk," Frank said.

"I love riding rodeo more than anything!" Randy exclaimed. "We just moved here last year, and I haven't made many friends. The rodeo is the first good thing that's happened to me since we got here."

"But why did you run away from us at the barbecue?" Frank asked.

"The deputy said you were detectives," Randy replied, "and I didn't want to be detected. Besides, my sponsor told me not to talk to anyone about the Seminole treasure. When someone stole the coin out of my locker, I didn't know who to trust."

"Your sponsor?" Frank thought aloud, as the answer came to him. "Salty Hubbard. The man you met through Trent Furman?"

"Yeah," Randy replied. "He was going to help me search for the rest of the treasure after the rodeo was over."

"Salty Hubbard, the charter-boat captain. Then I was right," Frank said. "The robbers didn't drown."

"What?" Randy couldn't see the connection. "How could those robbers have survived in those high seas after their airboat sank?"

"Because they weren't on it," Frank deduced. "The two robbers rendezvoused in Florida Bay with a bigger boat and a third accomplice—none other than Salty Hubbard."

14 Surprise Stowaways

"What makes you think Trent Furman will come to Salty Hubbard's boat?" Chet asked, munching on a candy bar. The long horseback ride from the rodeo grounds to the Frog's Peninsula Marina had made him hungry.

Joe and Chet had found a perfect hiding spot behind some crab traps stacked on the docks.

While he answered Chet's question, Joe kept his eyes glued to the *Hammerhead,* a deep-sea fishing boat that the dockmaster said belonged to Salty Hubbard. "When I was hiding in the swamp, two men walked by, searching for us," Joe recalled. "One voice was Zack Platt's, and I was so certain Trent Furman was his partner, I mistook the other voice to be his."

"But it was Salty Hubbard, the man in the white hat," Chet concluded. "Wow!" Chet's voice grew louder with his excitement. "So he's the one who sabotaged Dusty's hydroplane and who also left you stuck in the quicksand!"

"That's my guess," Joe replied.

"Still, Trent Furman must be involved," Chet added.

"I'm guessing he's the one who conked Barney Quick on the head and stole his costume," Joe said.

"But why would Trent Furman pose as a rodeo rider in the first place?" Chet wondered.

"So he could stay at the fishing camp near the lost gold and keep an eye on everyone," Joe said. "It also allowed him to roam anywhere on the rodeo grounds without seeming suspicious."

"And to pick Randy's lock in the bunkhouse," Chet ventured.

"Shh!" Joe suddenly warned his friend to quiet down. Hurrying past the dockmaster's shack and toward the slip where the *Hammerhead* was moored was none other than Trent Furman.

"He's going to board the *Hammerhead*," Chet whispered.

"Good," Joe whispered back. "So will we."

"Are you nuts?" Chet's whisper was more intense. "Why don't we just call the police?"

"We don't have enough proof to get them arrested," Joe explained. "For the police to start their own investigation, it would take days, and I don't think these crooks are planning to stick around much longer. We need to catch them red-handed."

Climbing out from behind the crab traps, they scurried down the dock past fishing vessels, sail-boats, and yachts until they reached the slip where the *Hammerhead* was moored.

Joe signaled Chet to stay low and out of the light coming from inside the cabin of the *Hammerhead.* Walking lightly up the gangplank, Joe stepped onto the deck.

The gangplank creaked loudly under Chet's heavy foot. Chet froze.

When no one emerged from the cabin to check on the noise, Joe motioned for Chet to come aboard. "Stay here," he whispered.

Joe got down on his knees and crawled along the outside of the main cabin until he could see through a lit window.

Trent Furman and Salty Hubbard appeared to be having a heated argument.

I've got to be able to hear what they're saying, Joe thought. Craning his neck to look around, he saw that the cabin door toward the rear of the boat had been left open.

He slipped quietly around the outside of the main cabin and crouched outside the open door.

"It's time to give up the search and make a run for it across the Gulf of Mexico," Joe overheard Furman telling Salty. "Those kids are on to us now, and after another storm hits Gator Swamp, we'll never be able to find those coins."

"If you hadn't been so careless leaving the sacks near the bow of the airboat," Salty retorted angrily, "we wouldn't have lost them overboard in the first place!"

"I'm a safecracker," Furman shouted back, "not a sailor or cowboy or treasure hunter!"

A voice transmission suddenly came over the shortwave radio. "This is Gatortail to *Hammerhead*," a deep voice announced. "I have located lost cargo and will have it on board in thirty minutes."

Furman and Hubbard's scowls turned to grins as Hubbard picked up the radio's hand receiver. "That's a big ten-four, Gatortail. Have you isolated the enemy camp? Over."

"The enemy camp is isolated," the voice on the radio reported, "and I left behind a little extra surprise for our young detectives."

Joe tried to decode their messages. The voice on the radio sounded like it belonged to Zack Platt, whose code name must be Gatortail. The lost cargo probably meant the gold coins. But what did Platt mean when he said, "The enemy camp is isolated," and what was the "extra surprise"? Joe wasn't sure he wanted to find out.

"Good work, Gatortail," Hubbard was saying. "We'll rendezvous in Florida Bay at the appointed spot. Over and out."

Hubbard put down the hand receiver and slipped on his white hat with the orange-and-black feather. As Salty turned toward the cabin door, Joe hurried toward the front of the boat. If he went down the gangplank to the dock, he knew he would be left out in the open and easily spotted.

He heard the familiar sound of a wood duck.

Jerking his head to the right, Joe saw Chet quacking and pointing frantically to a cargo hatch near where he was standing.

Chet opened the hatch, and the two boys dropped down into the storage area below. Joe and Chet stared wide-eyed and open-mouthed at the "cargo" being stowed there.

Bound and gagged in the cargo hold were Deputy Miles and Reuben Tallwalker!

Deputy Miles tried to say something through her gag, but Joe pointed upward and signaled her to keep quiet.

They sat still, listening to the footsteps of someone pacing back and forth on the deck above.

Joe waited until the footsteps had moved to the other end of the boat, then he and Chet began to untie Reuben and Deputy Miles.

"Boy, am I glad to see you two," the deputy said when her gag was off.

"How did you end up here?" Chet asked, as he began working on the ropes binding her feet.

"I'd forgotten to ask the dockmaster one important question," Deputy Miles explained. "All the boats in the harbor the night of the robbery were local. What I asked this afternoon was whether any of those local boats left port during the big squall."

"The *Hammerhead,*" Joe filled in.

"Bingo," the deputy replied. "I just came down to ask Salty Hubbard some routine questions about where he had gone in the middle of a squall. The next thing you know, he pulled a shotgun on me."

"I'm beginning to think he's the most ruthless one of the whole gang," Joe remarked.

"Gang?" Deputy Miles asked.

Reuben pulled his gag off with his free hand. "The alligator hunter, Platt. And the fisherman, Hubbard. When they caught me following them through the swamp, they tied me up, then Hubbard brought me here."

"There's a third robber. The safecracker is Trent Furman," Joe informed them.

"Who are they?" Reuben asked, still confused.

"They're the men who stole those rare gold coins from the vault in Miami," Joe replied.

"You're sure?" Deputy Miles asked.

"Almost dead certain," Joe said firmly.

"Let's get out of here and talk later," Chet said eagerly.

It was too late. The boat motor hummed to life at that moment. The stowaways could feel the boat moving away from the dock.

"Great," Chet grumbled.

"It's four against two," Reuben pointed out. "Pretty good odds."

"So Salty Hubbard loaned you his hat to hide your age?" Frank asked as he and Randy puttered along the shore of the bay toward Gator Swamp. "Our biggest riddle has the simplest answer."

"Yep. I forgot my hat at home the first day," Randy explained. "Salty said I looked like a young kid and an amateur without a hat, so he loaned me his for the night."

"And gave you the money to enter the other competition," Frank deduced.

"Right. But on the condition that I didn't tell anyone else about the gold coin I had found," Randy added.

"Where did you find the coin?" Frank asked.

"It'll be hard to pinpoint at night," Randy replied, "but I'll try to show you."

Randy manned the outboard motor, while Frank sat in the bow, acting as the lookout to keep them from hitting any stumps or heavy saw grass that would clog the propeller.

Finally they reached the island where the Hardys and Chet had been stranded.

"That's it, right?" Frank said. "Twin Cypress Key."

"No," Randy replied. "It's an island nearby that used to look like that."

"Used to?" Frank asked.

"You'll see what I mean," Randy said. A few minutes later, the boat rounded a bend. Just ahead was an island that looked like Twin Cypress Key, but Frank noticed there was one major difference.

"There's only one cypress tree," Frank said. Then he noticed a second cypress tree lying nearby, almost completely submerged under water. "The second tree was blown over in the squall!" Frank said.

"Right," Randy said. "Before the big storm, I used to have trouble telling these two islands apart."

"So the robbers have been looking in the wrong place this whole time," Frank deduced. "No wonder they haven't recovered the gold. Where exactly did you find the first coin?" he asked Randy.

"I found it there," Randy said, a slight quiver in his voice. "Right where that weird light is."

Frank saw the strange light beneath the surface of the water. He also spotted an airboat anchored about fifty feet away from the light.

"I can almost guarantee it's Zack Platt," Frank replied. "He must have figured out the riddle of the second cypress, too."

Frank signaled for Randy to cut the engine, and the two boys coasted up alongside the airboat. Frank spotted a shortwave radio on board as well as a wet canvas sack.

"Hey, what happened to the light?" Randy asked. In the brief moment that their attention was on the airboat, the light had vanished.

A hideous creature lunged out of the water behind Randy, grabbed him in a bear hug, then dragged him overboard into the swamp.

15 The Creature in the Swamp

"Randy!" Frank shouted, as he dove overboard to save him.

Under the black water, Frank began wrestling with the powerful creature. It had rubbery skin and large webbed feet. A man in a wet suit, Frank quickly realized.

Frank could not break the man's grip on Randy, but he was able to force him to the surface where he and Randy could at least catch a breath of air.

Tearing off the man's face mask, Frank confirmed what he had suspected. The man in the wet suit was Zack Platt.

For no apparent reason, Platt suddenly released Randy and swam away. Frank helped Randy back into the johnboat. Hanging off the side of the small craft, Frank scanned the water, waiting for Platt to attack again. But he was nowhere in sight.

"There!" Randy shouted, pointing over the bow of the johnboat. "He's climbing onto his airboat!"

Frank looked over to see Platt hauling a canvas sack aboard. "He's found the coins!" Frank shouted.

Platt started up his airboat and took off across Gator Swamp in the direction of Florida Bay. Randy yanked the pull cord to start his outboard motor, and they slowly began their pursuit.

Frank realized this was useless, and he shouted instructions to Randy. "Head for Dusty's fishing camp! Quick!"

Back on the *Hammerhead,* Joe searched the cargo hold for some makeshift weapons to use against their adversaries.

The sea was rough, and the boat rocked violently, making it hard for Chet to untie the last knot binding Deputy Miles's ankles.

"Find anything helpful, Joe?" Reuben asked, rubbing his sore rope-burned wrists.

"Nothing we could use for a weapon," Joe replied. "But look what I did find under these life jackets." Joe held up two black cloth hoods.

"Hoods?" Reuben asked, puzzled.

"The safecrackers wore black hoods," Deputy Miles recalled. "But how did they end up on this boat?"

"Somehow the robbers must have gotten word to Salty Hubbard that the police were chasing them," Joe began.

Chet jumped in with the answer. "A shortwave radio!"

"That's my hunch, too," Joe said. "Furman probably used the same shortwave that's now in his cabin at the fishing camp. They went with an alternate plan—to steal one of Angus Tallwalker's airboats and meet up in Florida Bay."

"But if they got away with the loot, why hang around here?" Deputy Miles asked.

"Chet and I figured they lost the coins overboard trying to get through Gator Swamp during the big squall," Joe explained.

"That's incredible!" Deputy Miles exclaimed. "If you boys want a job when you get out of high school, I hope you'll think of the Frog's Peninsula police force."

"Right now, I would be more concerned with being alive to graduate," Reuben interjected. "We need a plan to get out of here."

"Could we swim for it?" Chet asked.

"I don't know," Joe replied. "What's the shark situation in these waters?"

"There are a lot of them," Deputy Miles replied.

"Sharks probably wouldn't feed in this kind of weather," Reuben informed them.

"Well, that's good news," Joe said.

"On the other hand, in this kind of weather," Reuben added, "we would most likely all drown."

"If I could get to the shortwave radio, I could call for help," Joe said.

"Good idea," Deputy Miles said. "That seems to be our only hope."

"I'm going to let Reuben lead the way," Joe said. "If he can climb up a tree and paint messages on our foreheads without waking us, he can probably get us to the main cabin without being detected."

Reuben smoothly and silently opened the hatch a crack and looked out. "Hubbard is in the skipper's roost," he said. "I don't see Furman."

"Can we get by without being seen?" Joe asked.

Reuben didn't answer. He just sat watching, then suddenly said, "Now!"

Reuben jumped through the hatch and onto the deck in one swift movement. Joe did his best to keep up. They ducked behind the anchor just as Salty Hubbard turned his gaze back to the bow of the boat.

Crawling on their stomachs, the two boys moved along the deck and to the open door of the main cabin. Reuben peeked in, then motioned Joe forward. Joe climbed down two steps into the main cabin.

Another door was at the front of the cabin. Joe figured it led to the boat's sleeping quarters. The shortwave radio sat on a gray metal desk next to another device Joe realized was an electronic fish finder.

A detailed map of Gator Swamp with various islands marked off with red X marks was laid out on the desk. Dusty Cole's fishing camp was circled in black.

The shortwave radio made a high-pitched squeal as Joe switched it on. He turned the volume control to the lowest setting.

Reuben ducked his head into the cabin, signaling Joe to keep quiet. He disappeared for a moment, then reappeared, giving Joe the okay sign.

Joe picked up the hand receiver and pressed the button to transmit.

"Joe Hardy calling Cole's Fishing Camp," he said in a muffled whisper. There was no response, so he tried again, speaking a little louder. "This is Joe Hardy calling Cole's Fishing Camp." No one answered. Everyone must be asleep, Joe thought.

Just then a voice replied. "Howdy, Joe. I didn't know you were a ham operator."

Joe recognized Homer's voice. "Homer, we're in big trouble."

"You sure are. You woke me out of a dead sleep. Where are you? Over," Homer said.

"We're on Salty Hubbard's fishing boat," Joe replied.

"Fishing boat?" Homer blurted. "Don't you know there's a storm about to hit us?"

133

"Shh!" Joe tried to get Homer to lower his voice. "We've been trapped on board with the men who pulled the bank job in Miami. Over."

"Holy smoke!" Homer exclaimed.

"Shh! Tell Frank that we're on our way to meet up with Zack Platt. Over," Joe instructed Homer.

"Frank isn't here, and I'm afraid—" Homer's voice was suddenly cut off as someone switched off the shortwave radio.

"I was trying to catch a nap," Furman growled, pointing a thumb toward the sleeping quarters, "but you were making an awful racket out here."

"It's too late. I already sent an SOS to the police with our exact location," Joe said, bluffing.

Furman's eyes narrowed. "Good. Then they'll know exactly where to find your body after I've thrown you overboard."

"Not on your life!" Joe shouted as he pushed Furman, throwing him off balance long enough to make a break for the cabin door. Furman recovered quickly, though, lunging for Joe and tackling him to the floor.

Furman kneeled on Joe's back, pinning him down. "You lie still now, or I'll break every bone in your body," Furman threatened.

Reuben suddenly swung through the cabin door, hitting Furman squarely on the jaw and sending him flying backward.

Joe jumped to his feet and turned on Furman,

with Reuben by his side. "Two against one now," he said.

Furman wiped his bloody nose and eyed his two opponents.

"Hold it right there!" a voice behind Joe ordered. Joe and Reuben spun around to find themselves looking down the barrel of Salty Hubbard's shotgun. Furman quickly pulled a revolver from a drawer in the desk.

"Okay, you two, unless you want your friends here hurt, come on down nice and quiet," Hubbard called toward the open cabin door. Chet and Deputy Miles stepped into the cabin.

Hubbard snorted. "Well, well, Furman, it looks like we've got more shark bait than we figured on."

"Homer! Dusty!" Frank shouted as he ran into the darkness of the lodge at the fishing camp. He flipped the light switch. Nothing happened.

Frank stepped back outside, joined by Randy, who had grabbed the flashlight from his johnboat.

"The lights are out, and no one's inside. Let's try our cabin," Frank said, leading the way.

Rain and wind whipped the boys' faces as they ran past the row of cabins on stilts.

"This one," Frank called back to Randy as he bounded up the steps and into his cabin.

"Joe!" Frank shouted. As Randy entered and flashed the light around the cabin, a strange sight caught Frank's eye. He noticed a puddle of water on the floor with streaks of mud leading away from it. A large object beside the bed moved to block the path to the doorway with its head and the path to the window with its tail.

"F-F-Frank?" Randy stuttered. The beam of Randy's flashlight reflected off the milky white eye of a very long alligator.

"It's Big Bertha," Frank spoke calmly and quietly. "Okay, Randy, this is what we're going to do. We're going to circle around very slowly until we get behind her."

"I don't think I can move," Randy replied, a quiver in his voice.

"Then stand perfectly still," Frank instructed. Frank edged his way around the room toward the tail end of Big Bertha. He remembered what Steven Willow had said about an alligator's narrow field of vision.

"Now, Randy, in a few seconds I'm going to sit on Big Bertha's back," Frank explained.

"You're going to *what*?" Randy asked.

"I'm going to try to put her to sleep," Frank went on. "If it doesn't work, I want you to make a run for the door."

Big Bertha moved a few feet toward Randy. Frank knew he had to act quickly. Without making any sudden movements, he approached Big Bertha. In one smooth motion, Frank sat down, pushed the alligator's snout against the floor, and got a firm grip on it.

Big Bertha made a low growling sound. Frank held her jaws shut with a minimum amount of effort. This is just the way it worked for Mr. Willow, he thought.

"Frank!" Dusty shouted, flinging open the cabin door. It struck Big Bertha on the side of the head.

The giant alligator thrashed her tail and twisted her head. Frank hung on for dear life.

Dusty hopped onto Big Bertha with Frank, trying to keep the creature from rolling over and crushing them beneath its weight.

"Run!" Frank yelled to Randy. The alligator had moved enough for Randy to have a clear path to the screened window. Randy dove for the window, tearing out the screen and disappearing into the dark night outside.

Big Bertha was shaking her head violently from side to side, even though two large men were on her back, clutching her snout.

"I can't hold on much longer!" Frank told Dusty.

"Me either," the cowboy said.

Frank could hear the alligator's massive tail thrashing across the floor and saw it splinter a wooden chair against the wall.

"On the count of three, we'll both let go and make a run for the window!" Frank shouted.

Dusty began the count. "One . . . two . . .

three!" At the same moment, Frank and Dusty released Big Bertha's snout, backpedaled away, and rushed toward the window. The monster alligator swung her head around and snapped her jaws shut, just missing Frank's right foot.

Dusty jumped out the window headfirst, somersaulting and landing awkwardly on his shoulder. Frank hopped sideways through the window, leading with his feet. He held on to the window ledge for a split second before dropping, lessening the impact of his fall.

Randy was on his hands and knees on the ground, gasping for air. "I'm fine," he said to Frank as he stood up.

"Dusty, how are you doing?" Frank asked.

"I have ridden fifty wild bulls, a hundred wild horses, and one big mama alligator without being hurt," Dusty replied. "And I think I just broke my arm jumping out of that little window."

Homer arrived on the scene, grumbling about his pontoon boat. "Someone's done a real number on it. Sabotaged the engine. We're stranded here like a one-legged cat in a redwood tree."

Frank quickly told Homer what had happened. The older man and the two boys gently got Dusty to his feet and helped him toward the lodge.

"Someone rigged the generator to short-circuit," Dusty said. "Homer and I were out back fixing it when we heard you calling."

"Let's worry about you for now, Dusty," Frank said.

"That's a luxury we don't have," Dusty said, with a worried look to Homer. "Tell him."

"Your brother radioed in just before the generator went out," Homer told Frank. "He and Chet are trapped on Salty Hubbard's charter boat. We were cut off before Joe could give me the location."

"We don't need a location," Frank said. "If we follow Zack Platt, he'll lead us right to them."

"Follow him how, Frank?" Randy asked. "You said yourself, the only way we'll catch him is in another airboat, and now he's got a ten-minute head start on us."

Frank shook his head. Randy was right.

"Give Homer another five minutes, and he'll have the generator fixed," Dusty said. "We'll radio the Coast Guard."

Frank nodded.

The rest of the guests had been awakened by the commotion, and they were arriving at the lodge, carrying lanterns and wearing rain gear.

"I can set that arm until we get you to a hospital," Billy Biggs offered.

"And I've got some medicine that'll ease the pain," Homer added.

Dusty nodded yes to both offers. Frank stepped outside the lodge and away from the crowd to have a moment to think.

The wind gusted powerfully, pounding the heavy rain into Frank's face, but he hardly noticed. His brother and friend were in trouble, and he felt helpless to do anything.

"I'm sorry, Frank," Randy said, having followed him outside.

"Thanks," Frank replied.

Now, over the sound of the wind, Frank thought he heard something. The rumble of an engine. A sound he recognized. "The hydroplane!"

16 A Last Hope from the Sky

Looking up, Frank spotted the plane's running lights as the small craft, buffeted by the high winds, made its approach to land beside Cole's Key.

The hydroplane shuddered as it touched down on the rough water. Frank ran to the dock, meeting Steven Willow as he climbed out of the cockpit.

"Dusty owes me a favor," Willow said. "In fact, he owes me a hundred favors. That was the roughest trip I've ever taken."

"What are you doing here?" Frank asked, wiping the rain away from his eyes.

"I got some disturbing news this evening," Willow said. "For your sake, I couldn't risk *not* coming."

"What do you mean?" Frank wondered.

"A friend in Big Cypress told me all about Zack Platt," Willow began. "Platt just finished serving a nine-month jail sentence for alligator poaching. He made friends with another prisoner, some guy who was a safecracker."

"Trent Furman," Frank said.

"Yeah, how did you know?" Willow asked.

"It's a long story," Frank replied. "And we have zero time to spare. My brother and Chet are trapped on a boat with a pair of cutthroats."

"You're not thinking about flying in this weather?" Willow warned. "I was crazy to get here, and the storm is getting worse by the minute!"

"I don't care!" Frank shouted back.

"Frank, where's Dusty?" Willow asked. "If anyone should try flying in this weather, it's him."

"Dusty broke—" Randy began to reply.

"He's in the lodge," Frank blurted out, cutting off Randy. Willow nodded, then headed toward the lodge.

"What was that all about?" Randy asked. "You know that Dusty's in no condition to fly."

"Yeah," Frank replied, "I also know that he and Mr. Willow would never risk letting *me* fly."

Frank climbed into the cockpit. The keys to the hydroplane were still in the ignition.

"You're going up in this thing?" Randy asked.

"Randy, I don't think Joe and Chet have a prayer if we don't get to that boat before Zack Platt does."

"Then I'm going with you," Randy insisted.

"You know how to fly?" Frank asked.

Randy shrugged. "No. But it'll be safer than you going up alone." Before Frank could protest, Randy climbed into the copilot's seat.

Frank headed the hydroplane directly into the wind to give it lift. He pushed it full throttle, trying to pick up enough speed to take off. Even in the swamp, the water was rough, and the plane shuddered as it bumped along the surface.

"Hang on," Frank told Randy, as he pulled up gently on the controls. The hydroplane lifted off the water and soared upward, pushed by the oncoming wind.

"Keep your eyes peeled for Platt's boat!" Frank shouted to Randy, over the roar of the engine and the howl of the wind outside.

"Got him!" Randy shouted back, pointing off to the right.

The airboat had been slowed by the heavy seas. Frank spotted its destination about half a mile ahead. "Running lights!" he shouted to Randy. "Looks like a large boat! That one must be Hubbard's boat."

Frank brought the hydroplane in low to get a good look at the fishing boat. Two men were pushing four other figures toward the rear of the vessel. A moment later the two men threw all four of their captives off the back of the boat and into the raging sea.

"They tossed them overboard!" Frank shouted to Randy. "I'm circling around. We're going to pick them up."

"Okay, Frank," Randy replied.

Frank focused his mind on everything he had learned from Dusty about piloting the plane. He would have to land the small craft in a choppy sea and a raging wind. "Hang on," he said to Randy.

Frank had the wind behind him now, and he was able to keep the plane level in spite of a few sudden crosswinds. The pontoons touched down in the trough between two large swells, but vaulted up into the air again when it hit the crest.

Frank kept a firm grip on the controls. The initial impact slowed them down enough so that when he touched down the second time, he was able to bring the craft to a successful halt.

Waves lashed against the side of the aircraft, rocking it until it nearly tipped over.

Opening the hatch of the cockpit and stepping out onto a pontoon, Frank saw Joe, Chet, Reuben, and Deputy Miles bobbing in the water about fifty yards away. They seemed to be having great difficulty keeping their heads above water.

"Their hands must be tied," Frank told Randy. "I'm going after them."

"I'm going with you!" Randy insisted, climbing out onto the other pontoon.

They dove into the bay. Frank was so pumped

144

with adrenaline that he reached his brother in less than a minute.

"I'm all right," Joe yelled to Frank. "Get Chet first!"

Chet was another twenty feet away. His head kept dropping below the surface, and he was swallowing a lot of water.

Frank tried to put Chet in a lifeguard hold, but Chet protested. "Cut the ropes, Frank. Don't risk leaving the others out here while you take me back to the plane."

Frank reached into his back pocket, relieved to find he had not lost his penknife. He quickly began cutting through the rope binding Chet's wrists, until they finally gave way and snapped.

Frank could see that Randy was already halfway back to the hydroplane with Deputy Miles. "Where's Reuben?" Frank asked as he began cutting his brother's ropes.

Joe scanned the area, but Reuben was nowhere to be seen. Once loose from his ropes, the younger Hardy began swimming away from the plane, hoping to find his new friend.

Frank grabbed his brother by the collar. "If Reuben went under, we'll never find him at night in these rough seas!" Frank yelled, tugging Joe back toward the plane. "And I'm not going to lose you in the process!"

Joe reluctantly swam back toward the hydroplane

with Frank. Randy and Deputy Miles helped Frank aboard.

On the passenger side of the plane, Joe was also offered a hand up onto the pontoon. His mouth dropped open as he looked into the face of Reuben Tallwalker. "Reuben! How did you get back?"

"It was Seminole magic." Reuben grinned. "Actually, it's called the dolphin stroke. It's sort of like the butterfly, but with no hands."

Joe laughed, giving Reuben a friendly slap on the shoulder. Suddenly a gunshot sent up a spray of water a few feet behind them.

Fifty yards away, Joe saw Zack Platt standing on the bow of his airboat. The second blast from his double-barreled shotgun tore through the left pontoon.

"Get in!" Frank shouted.

Everyone crammed into the small cockpit of the hydroplane. The last one in was Chet. "I hope this thing will fly with so many people in it."

"We've got more trouble," Deputy Miles said, pointing through the windshield. Hubbard's boat, the *Hammerhead*, had turned about and was headed back in their direction.

"What's he doing?" Chet asked.

Joe's eyes widened. "He's going to ram us!"

"Not if I can help it!" Frank said, starting the engine. He opened the throttle and began picking up speed.

The *Hammerhead* veered to the right, trying to block their path.

"We'll never pull up in time," Deputy Miles warned.

"I know what I'm doing," Frank said reassuringly, then took a deep breath.

Joe saw Platt reloading his shotgun. The *Hammerhead* was directly ahead. "Frank, you need to make this happen soon."

Frank nodded, though he was just short of a safe takeoff speed. He pulled back on the controls lightly, and the nose of the aircraft rose just as a shotgun blast struck the surface of the water below them.

Frank saw Furman duck his head as the hydroplane cleared the deck of the *Hammerhead* by a few feet.

"Yahoo!" Randy hollered as the plane continued ascending. "This is better than riding Volcano!"

Looking below, Joe saw Furman and Hubbard hauling the sacks of gold coins off the airboat. "Boy, I hate seeing those crooks get away."

"They won't get away, Joe," Reuben stated firmly.

"You sound awfully sure," Chet noted in awe. "Can you see the future?"

"No," Reuben replied. "I can see the Coast Guard boat out of my side of the airplane."

Frank saw it, too. A Coast Guard cutter moved in

quickly on the gang of bank robbers. The cockpit rocked with laughter. It wasn't until the laughter died down that Joe thought of something. "Hey, Frank. Do you know how to land this thing?"

"I'm one for one so far," Frank replied calmly. Turbulence made the small craft rise up and swoop down suddenly. The cockpit grew very quiet.

The lights from the fishing camp came into view. "Brace yourselves," Frank instructed. "It's going to be a little rough."

A moment later one pontoon struck the top of the water hard, then bounced up, slamming the other pontoon against the water as if it were the other end of a seesaw. The craft lofted up, rising over the dock of the fishing camp, then touched down on solid land and went into a slide. Joe closed his eyes. Chet and Randy were hollering at the top of their lungs.

Finally the hydroplane came to a halt. The cockpit was quiet again except for the sound of heavy breathing and sighs of relief.

When Joe opened his eyes, he had to laugh. To each side of the plane were two stilts. They had come to rest directly below the Hardys' cabin. "Boy, am I glad you didn't knock our cabin off its stilts."

"If you knew who was trapped inside our cabin," Frank replied, smiling, "you would *really* be glad." Frank and Randy burst into laughter. Joe, Reuben, and Deputy Miles just looked at each other and shrugged.

The storm passed through that night, and by one o'clock the next day, the sun was shining in a clear blue sky as if nothing had ever happened.

Sitting in the grandstands at the rodeo, nursing their bumps and bruises, Joe and Frank saw cowboy after cowboy compete in the dangerous sport of wild-bull riding. "I'm glad to be watching *other* people face danger for a change," Joe said to his brother.

Frank smiled. "I'm glad Trent Furman, Salty Hubbard, and Zack Platt are safely in jail."

"To tell you the truth, I'll be happy to get back to Bayport and solid ground," Joe said. "The next time I get wet, I want it to be because I jumped under a shower."

The boys watched Reuben ride Nightmare to victory in the bull-riding competition. Dusty's right arm was in a sling, and Mr. Deeter refused to let him enter that event, no matter how much the Hardys' daredevil-friend protested.

Dusty settled for the two-man steer-roping competition. He and his partner, Homer, charged after the steer as it raced out of the chute into the ring.

Homer lassoed the steer's back hooves and Dusty lassoed it around the head. Homer backed his horse away, keeping the steer from moving. One-handed, Dusty jumped off his horse, grabbed the steer by the horns, and twisted until it dropped onto its side. The crowd applauded wildly.

"Now, there's one for the record books." Frank nudged his brother as he applauded. "Steer roping with one arm in a sling."

Dusty let the steer up, and Barney Quick removed the ropes. Dusty waved his hat to the crowd, offering his thanks.

"Here are Randy Stevens and Chet Martin," Mr. Deeter announced over the public-address system.

"Chet *Morton*," Chet called toward the announcer's box from the back of his horse.

"Can you believe it?" Frank said, grinning. "Chet's actually going through with this."

"I'm surprised Randy's dad is letting him ride," Joe replied.

"Mr. Stevens was so proud of Randy for helping us solve this mystery, he said he could participate in any event that allowed a fourteen-year-old to compete," Frank explained.

Barney Quick opened the chute, and the steer ran out. Randy caught the steer and lassoed its back leg in a snap. Chet was only a few seconds behind, lassoing the steer's horns on his first try.

Chet jumped down off the horse and grabbed the steer by the horns. The Hardys exchanged surprised glances. Unfortunately, the steer was not giving up. It swung its head up and down, bouncing Chet along with it.

Finally Chet brought the steer to the ground. Exhausted, he waved his hat to the crowd while sitting in the dirt.

The Hardys laughed heartily. But when they heard only a smattering of applause from the other spectators, they rose to their feet and cheered loudly, leading a standing ovation for their two brave friends.

SPOOKSVILLE

R·L·STINE'S
GHOSTS OF FEAR STREET®

1 HIDE AND SHRIEK   52941-2/$3.99
2 WHO'S BEEN SLEEPING IN MY GRAVE? 52942-0/$3.99
3 THE ATTACK OF THE AQUA APES 52943-9/$3.99
4 NIGHTMARE IN 3-D   52944-7/$3.99
5 STAY AWAY FROM THE TREE HOUSE 52945-5/$3.99
6 EYE OF THE FORTUNETELLER 52946-3/$3.99
7 FRIGHT KNIGHT   52947-1/$3.99
8 THE OOZE   52948-X/$3.99
9 REVENGE OF THE SHADOW PEOPLE 52949-8/$3.99
10 THE BUGMAN LIVES!   52950-1/$3.99
11 THE BOY WHO ATE FEAR STREET   00183-3/$3.99
12 NIGHT OF THE WERECAT   00184-1/$3.99
13 HOW TO BE A VAMPIRE   00185-X/$3.99
14 BODY SWITCHERS FROM OUTER SPACE 00186-8/$3.99
15 FRIGHT CHRISTMAS   00187-6/$3.99
16 DON'T EVER GET SICK AT GRANNY'S   00188-4/$3.99
17 HOUSE OF A THOUSAND SCREAMS   00190-6/$3.99

 Available from Minstrel® Books
Published by Pocket Books

POCKET
B O O K S

NANCY DREW® MYSTERY STORIES By Carolyn Keene

A MINSTREL® BOOK
Published by Pocket Books